I0556575

BAD ACTORS
Adventures in the Liaden Universe® Number 33
Sharon Lee and Steve Miller

1

BAD ACTORS
Adventures in the Liaden Universe® Number 33

• • • •

Pinbeam Books: pinbeambooks.com

• • • •

• • • •

"EXCERPTS FROM TWO LIVES" first appeared in *Star Destroyers*, Baen Books, March 2018

"Dark Secrets" first appeared in *Infinite Stars: Dark Frontiers*, Titan, November 2019

"Revolutionists" first appeared in *The Razor's Edge*, Zombies Need Brains, June 2018

• • • •

COVER DESIGN BY: SELFPUBBOOKCOVERS.com/ billwyc
ISBN: 978-1-948465-18-2

The authors thank the following Fearless Tyop Hunters:
Christina Larson
Sheila Oranch
Sarah Stapleton

Dedicated to Liaden readers, past, present, and in future

Note from the Authors

WE HOPE YOU'LL FORGIVE our expectation that if you're reading this you probably have a passing or even more than passing acquaintance with the the Liaden Universe®, a universe that we—Sharon Lee and Steve Miller—have been writing in since the 1980s. One set of our business cards says: *The Liaden Universe®, where honor, wit, and true love are potent weapons against deceit and treachery.* Well, given that, it probably comes as no surprise that a lot of our stories focus on people of honor and wit who love truly. Many of our readers applaud this—and expect it. Still, the yin yang of life, the dialectic of story, necessity, in fact, requires that somewhere in the Liaden experience there must be opponents of honor, wit, and true love, or at least people with surprising takes on what those means. You probably know that.

If you're a regular reader of our work, you probably know more than what we write; you know something of our methods and how we stay in touch with our readers and fans. So if you're a regular reader, you may be surprised by this chapbook appearing at all, much less now.

But see, **Bad Actors** came as a surprise to us, too. A surprise even though we're the proprietors of Pinbeam Books and nothing happens at Pinbeam without us. We usually plan when the next chapbook will come out, with Sharon making careful notes on our calendar—sometimes even the two-year calendar! – and with an eye to making sure as many of our readers have access to our stories as possible.

Given that some of our readers only want to purchase from particular vendors, or don't want to purchase from particular vendors, or want things only electronically, or only in paper, making stories available in Pinbeam chapbooks gives us a way reach our readers where they want to be reached. Since some of our chapbooks contain originals, you the reader are used to our work appearing just as soon as it can. Sigh . . . not this time, friends.

In this case, though, **Bad Actors** snuck up on us, a result of anthology publishing schedules, reprints in other venues, and contracts requiring exclusivity for varying terms. In some cases, we cannot reprint before a hardcover edition has a soft-cover counterpart, in others we're required to wait for a full six months, or a full year, or a full *eighteen months* after a story first appears. Given that sometimes stories are held for anthologies for months or years, it can make it hard to recall which story appeared where and when, and which are due to pass through the Pinbeam Books chapbook process.

So timing came into play, as did authorial forgetfulness. In the midst of the pandemic we were so focused on moving forward that we let go of the fact that several stories had yet to reach the chapbook stage, though they'd been seen elsewhere.

In a way we were lucky that the three Liaden Universe® stories in **Bad Actors** blend themselves into a theme as they do, that the editorial commissioning of stories meant that the stories lent themselves to the cover art so convincingly. We won't study too hard on the coincidence of so many editors looking for hard-edged stories where the story centered around bad actors and hard decisions . . . but they did.

Here then are three stories for your delectation.

"Excerpts From Two Lives," first appeared in passing as a song—"The Ballad of the RosaRing"—in our Liaden novel *Carpe*

Diem, published in 1989. "Excerpts . . . " first appeared in the Baen anthology *Star Destroyers* in March of 2018.

"Dark Secrets," was commissioned for the Titan Books anthology *Infinite Stars: Dark Frontiers* which came out in November of 2019.

"Revolutionists" which was first published in June of 2018 in *The Razor's Edge* anthology from Zombies Need Brains LLC.

We hope you'll enjoy them if this is your first reading and enjoy re-reading if you've seen them before.

Even Bad Actors need to be seen sometimes!

• • • •

SHARON LEE AND STEVE Miller, Cat Farm and Confusion Factory, June 2021

Excerpts from Two Lives

AVERIL 21, 407 CONFEDERATION Standard Year

"Beam Banks One and Two, go live as leads. We have identified and targeted a threat. Prepare to fire on my command, on radar's central target. This is not a drill, you will go to full combat power. Saturate the disc at all wavelengths."

Proper quiet, proper response. The ship's routine went on but the air circulators changed speed, and life-support panels grew angry red as combat-power overrides initiated. Small bells echoed the necessities of combat: hatches, airlocks, and pressure doors sealed.

"Combat power up." Nerves in that voice, but it didn't squeak.

"Lead banks, we'll need three consecutive full-power bursts from each—lock that in! Bank Three, slave to Bank One, two point seven five second delay, wide angle. Bank Four, slave to Bank Three, ultrawide angle. Banks Five through Twelve, go to high alert. Missilery Section, watch for bulk breakaway going in-system, target at will. Section leaders, you will particularly react to bulk breakaway coming our way."

The crew shared glances. They'd deviated, on captain's orders, from what was to be a calm and peaceful direct rendezvous with the RosaRing.

Meteor shields went live automatically. The target was a little over a tenth of a light-second away, so energetic debris wasn't an immediate threat.

The captain said nothing, watching this crew's first live-fire action. The sub-captain was sweating: His experience on this system was simulations. His battle experience had been on ships

9

whose entire beam output was negligible compared to any single projector in any of the battleship's twenty multibeam projector banks. There was a reason these beams were called planet busters, as they were about to prove.

Radar showed the target, distance and rotation. Like many planets, there was ice at the poles. Like many planets there was atmosphere. Like many planets, one might target the broadside equator, where rotational stress assisted the destructive effects of incoming beams.

The captain and the sub-captain had spent several sessions in the captain's cabin perfecting this plan. The crew thought it merely the third drill, but the target *was* a danger to Trikandle; the sub-captain had done the math the captain required.

The sub-captain's orders from the captain: develop an attack sequence, prepare the crew through drills, and then give the deck commands required for the kill, on the captain's signal. The captain required excellence from those who served under him.

In return, in those sessions, he displayed excellence. He'd shared the words and codes of exigency—the ship's self-destruct sequence, the code of relinquishing command, the codes for . . . all of them. Smit had taught him, and he passed the ship's necessities on.

The captain listened to the deck, the radar, the hum of power that underlay the deck, the stars beyond, just as he'd seen Admiral Smit listen. The form was Admiral Smit's axiom: Effective command radiates power; those under command bask in the rays of their orders.

Watching the screens, feeling the universe flow around him, the captain radiated command, looking firmly at the sub-captain and saying "*Ni faris*," into the mic that reached only the sub-captain's headset.

A startle there, a so brief pause. The sub-captain's glance fled from the captain's face to his command screen, and he echoed the captain to his crew. "We commit! Fire!"

The deck thrummed and the power was an audible rasp ending in a noise that was. . .

"Zap!"

The sotto voce comment by a crewman unseen barely beat the squeal of discharge that thrummed the entire fabric of the battleship. On screens crew throughout the ship saw what happens when a bank of planet-buster projectors hurls the forces of chaos.

The captain blinked. Some teaching moments have more impact than others. When he'd accepted this mission on that Day of Changes, when he'd last held Verita in their own bed, he hadn't expected to train a crew so raw, nor to have orders on file permitting such a mission. Things were going well, seventeen days in system.

Change Year Day, Sumtap 01, 404 CSY

They'd begun that Day of Changes knowing there *would be* changes.

This was not their first Day of Changes; they'd learned the meaning of it together as child scholars, learned the joy of festive food and guessing games, learned later of the small pains that might come from the day, then, the larger ones as schoolmates and first crushes were pared away by the necessities of more adult pursuits.

Eventually they'd pled their cases one to another for more than stolen kisses and learned to trust in each other's hard-driving ambition. They turned to each other rather than others, asking "How do we solve this?" or, admitting being at wit's end: "Solve this!" They wore matching bands of custom Triluxian in honor of their plans.

His ambition led him to the fleet, in search of opportunity as it recovered from the debacle of the Battle of Azren Clouds. He'd risen quickly, leading several raiding missions and rescues before being attached to Admiral Smit and *Implacable*.

She, drawn to research, joined the efforts to extract the most dangerous secrets of the Ligonier Library, where her skills at academic infighting were as recognized as her scientific insights. Nor had Verita shared all her solvings with the academic community, reserving for herself and Kiland the news that she'd moved from theory to actual practice several strains of those life-constructions thought lost in the collapsed universe their foremothers had fled.

While the old guard flailed at the changes wrought by dusty carbon clouds invading their trade lanes, Kiland and Verita shone as beacons for the future. Let the failures retire or suicide—they dealt only in power and success.

On that memorable Day of Change, they played before the clock buzzed them officially into the dawn. Verita began by nipping his ear and spooning him, her hands busy, mouth full of kisses and words; promises, teases—and *more*, her potent arms pulling his shoulder, aiming his willing mouth and . . .

After, they sat in their atrium, cheered by their nakedness as ocean breezes brought them spring's promise of more than mere renewal. What sprang from this year would crown their lives.

By tradition, they arrived at dusk, he from the south, she from the north, at their own front door. Flowers and gifts they each carried in profusion, the promise of change strong in their hands while their faces were a little secret, the mouths a little sad under the smiles.

"I will be your slave tonight, my love," said Verita, as they exchanged delicate fragrant bouquets on their threshold. "And you will solve my passion.

"Unless," she added, as she followed him into their home, "unless you demand I solve for you, in which case I will take tomorrow."

"Slave or solve." He laughed. "I'll savor either."

He trembled with lust, though they were still dressed, and his eyes darkened his smile. But her smile, too, was near fled, dancing on the tip of her tongue.

"Is it well, *Katido Volupto*?" he whispered, and shed his burdens as she shed hers, the hall table not large enough for the wealth of gifts they had brought.

"It is," she said. "It is so well it is nearly perfect. The project goes forward . . . yes. But until it is announced, I can hardly tell you more. And for you?"

"Yes, it is nearly perfect. Next week, I return to space!"

She laughed, and was relieved, nearly knocking him down as she wrapped herself about him, filling his eyes with her kisses and his ears with her demand, "Tell me, tell me that you will not be lonely. Next week I go to space, as well!"

Averil 04, 407 CSY

Implacable in a hurry was a sight to be seen, which was good, since there was no way of hiding the fearsome output of its antique power units. The mighty timonium plasma sets spewed neutrons and neutrinos alike while powering the last ship of the line from any of the Cloudgate armed forces. She left behind an elemental thermal signature that might cloud an astronomer's view of the cosmos for centuries, but the chance of there being such, here, was negligible.

Ship of the line was a misnomer when applied to *Implacable*, for most ships of its type fielded two centuries ago were gone. Of that generation of *batalsipo grandas*—a dozen dozen ships more powerful than entire modern star fleets—only *Implacable* held air. The others were victims of their wars or, as often, dismantled for resources.

Verita watched the secret news of *Implacable's* arrival. Station Ops was slow in this; her own equipment better tuned—she'd had budget for new installs while Ops was stuck with original equipment. So much of the mission was on scant budget, including using the mighty *Implacable* as a towboat! However, the calculations had worked well for the incoming trip, with the transit from Jump point to Trikandle's one-hundred-day orbit a mere twelve days. This time *Implacable* was too awkwardly placed for such a quick run, she knew.

Kiland's Change Day news had placed him back aboard the vessel that had made him one of the most powerful men in the reformed Confederation. The same Change Day saw Verita leap to her life-long goal—science leader of an expedition that could return the Confederation to greatness.

As principal investigator she was technically second-in-command of the RosaRing, an agricultural lab repurposed into a self-sufficient xenoplanet research laboratory. The administrator's position was higher in the flow charts, but Prenla Verita was the reason the RosaRing had been dispatched.

Among the last messages from *Implacable* as it departed the system had been several for her, under admiral's seal—sent by Kiland, with Admiral Smit's approval. Each was more full of promise than the last, and the final promising what they'd suspected: Smit was retiring, and he favored as commander of *Implacable* none but Kiland.

Now orbiting the fecund planet Trikandle, the real mission of the RosaRing was daunting: hurry Trikandle through an evolution toward the oxygenated photosynthetic atmosphere required to add it as a populated Confederation world. This was hands-on work—with satellites, imaging systems, drones, rovers, and observer craft.

The Confederation's directors had risked much in mounting the expedition at all, and they'd cast for glory over stability, rushing their claim on the Trikandle system by making the station a permanent fixture.

The atmosphere on Trikandle was an unbreathable amalgam: storms of methane mixing with unstable compounds, leaving odd pools of multilayered liquids . . . including water. Measurable pockets of oxygen enriched the atmosphere in deep valleys and craters. It was now oxygen rich for a world where free oxygen had hitherto been bound to rocks or was a trace gas high in the atmosphere.

On Trikandle life roiled, it flittered, it rolled; it gathered itself into mats of color and motion, it launched itself against barriers of other life with potent chemistry of acid and base. It grew through ceaseless life cycles of solution and dissolution. As it writhed into toxic tentacles, grew sniffer stalks and eye puddles, it fed a future Verita was struggling to direct.

Verita was supported by the work she'd done since graduate school, fed by secrets pilfered in the great war more than a century gone by, when *Implacable*'s weapons led the attack on Quadraterra's defenses and stood guard over the looting of the Ligonier Library.

Some of that looted knowledge had been useless; the physics of a closed and finite universe did not translate perfectly to this one. But in the end times of the old universe, there'd been clones and all manner of living abominations shaped by the unknowable minds of the Great Enemy, *Sherikas*. That there were detailed instructions of the building of such pseudolife was a secret Verita held close.

Scientists at Ligonier Library had plotted their control of the new universe, using the tools that had won the old. They'd been pushed to unleash at-will terraforming, wild cellular advances—and much of their knowledge had come to Verita's hands.

Verita's ambition supported Kiland's. They were a good team politically and would carry their bloodlines to the top of the Confederation's hierarchy. Well-placed by birth and education, they would easily live two centuries or more. Their Confederation would sweep aside the remnants of the old Terran Empire, the Liadens, and even the Yxtrang.

In Verita's display screens *Implacable*'s thrust sparkled across many bands, infernos created by in-system engines that were no longer welcome in most habited systems.

The Confederation's pride and joy . . . well, once there was a new source of accessible wealth under their control, a whole new planet to be used, followed by many more to be farmed at will—then, *Implacable* could be a regal exemplar of their might!

Kiland's parting message going out she knew by heart, and believed it still:

"I live to serve your needs and solve your problems, my Verita. Our next Change Day together we shall reprise and surmount all our dreams and fantasies."

And now—*Implacable* was back, and all of their future beckoned.

• • • •

IT WAS THE SIXTH HUNDREDTH day since the special pair of rovers was unleashed.

Today, Verita studied the area called Quozmo. The implication of the new, bolder streaking on ground and air was clear to her, though she really wished to be sure it was not yet clear to Admin Desler. Admin was only a few days returned from her course of enforced rest. In other days her episode might have been called "nervous exhaustion." Admin's work had become more difficult with the several suicides among the staff overworked with aging equipment and shredded schedules. Desler, a tenured academic appointed to the post to remove her from a politically sensitive position, was unequal to the increased stress.

It had taken time for the crew psychologist to understand the situation and by then, Admin Desler had been in a precarious state. She was taken under care, some of her work redistributed to Verita and to Desler's assistant.

The right corner of the screen showed a notification—ground side ops. She gestured and took the voice call.

"Investigator, I've a message from Quozmo Ob2. They've lost relay from the Debae and Dabbie rover pair again and they're down to four drones, three of them lightweights. Do we want the drones all back now?"

Verita pushed back at her hair—if Kiland didn't prefer it long enough to brush and caress she'd have cut it short.

"Condense the last of the valley images and send them to me. Begin reacquisition interrogation on the rovers. Work on that, priority!"

The rover teams . . . the rover teams acted like they were sentient. They weren't, of course, Verita never quite dared bringing both parts of the legacy together. Though for this, she had considered it.

The rovers *were* semi-autonomous. They could go for years without input—collecting, analyzing, reporting when queried. The pair's self-selected braided trail method was working so well she'd asked the next units be programmed to emulate it. The lead rovers were encountering pods and accumulations of . . . things. Life. New life. Life chosen and sown by her will, growing in a wilderness of chaos.

The valley the rovers roamed was a tectonic artifact, more a long gash than a crater. The upthrust of plateau at the far end looked to be impact residue, but her studies confirmed the heights as cooling volcanic plumes, recent. Those plumes generated thermal activity in the valley, a rich source of energy and minerals. Minerals including timonium, platinum, gold.

The valley was geologically active, with three rivers rushing into it. The hydrocarbons were interesting, but one of those rivers ran seasonally as water, as it did now, sometimes sharing the riverbeds, sometimes competing. Within the last year, spongy mats of winter vegetation had begun catching against the cliffsides, and the oxygen levels were notably higher.

"Yes," Verita said to ground ops, "recover the drones, as long as they haven't been below the pressure threshold."

"Altitude threshold, right, not height threshold? We've been pushing, as you requested. There's been wind and updrafts around the mount—we've been using that to keep the glidefoils active beyond normal duration."

Verita closed her eyes, considering. Yes, she'd approved that. There shouldn't have been any problem there, surely . . .

"Show me the flight paths. Show me recent weather, too."

As those screens came up, simultaneously there was a shout from somewhere down the hall and a chime.

The admin's voice rang out throughout the RosaRing.

"Attention, all staff. We have a distant Jump arrival confirmed and are awaiting ID. Scan Security, please man your stations. Timing is appropriate for our Year Three Rendezvous."

Verita grinned, even though she'd known. She had so much to share with Kiland, doubtless he for her.

In the meantime, she had a decision to make.

She leaned back, sniffing at the flight paths now on screen as if she could scent a hint of ammonia, or of the crystalline precipitate which sometimes wafted to the gravel beds left behind after the flush of spring floods.

The pressure gradients were in flux. The stronger of the atmospheric currents had tunneled through the flat current they called the mesostream, which sometimes held considerable water vapor. The visualization showed a convective dance then, as if ramped high into the sky by the volcanic uplands, high into the stratopause.

Technically, the drones were not to fly as low as the stratopause, where the temperatures neared the freezing point of water. In such conditions microbes might be found on normal worlds.

Verita made her decision.

"Call them home."

Averil 04, 407 CSY

"What's the measure on that? Are we even at the right star? Where's the gassers?"

Kiland's sarcasm was inappropriate if nearly inaudible.

Automatics admitted that yes, *Implacable* had come to the right place despite her recalcitrant Struven units and the haste of their departure. The gas giants rolled in their orbits, the companion brown dwarf continued its distant, lonely journey three quarters of a light-year away among rocky clouds of debris. *He* read them that quickly, but his crew . . .

His crew checked their instruments, followed protocol, eventually they nodded at him.

He signaled the traditional arrival announcement. It went out without the usual time-to-dock though, and he . . . did the math himself, signaling the sub-captain to do the same.

"Shield at basic," he said, but the automatics were seeing to that, the junior officers chasing behind, just in case.

"Weapons checks, threats?"

There were no threats.

At full in-system power it would take them days just to overcome the fractional errors; right now they were moving at significant velocity *away* from their target. The revamped crew was still learning the ship—Admiral Smit's veteran crew would never have arrived so far off the mark, or so unsure of the recover.

"Attention, *Implacable*, we are arrived and making our way to the RosaRing. This will not be a twelve-day jaunt; expect full maintenance routines. Deck officers set duty cycles. Acceleration alerts within the hour."

Kiland looked to the sub-captain.

"Three channels, in the clear, Captain. The time signals are there, but no space weather roundups. The orbital elements are automatic, but the star observation reports ought to be continuous."

"Record what's there, get us synced, ask for what's missing. Send captain's regards to the RosaRing's Trikandle Expedition. Tell them we're bringing treasures from home. Once comm schedules are established, send and request the archives. In the meanwhile, let us compare projected courses, shall we? We have work to do."

Averil 05, 407 CSY

From Principal Investigator via RosaRing Secure COMM 7 for Captain's Eyes Only

Point A: My joy and strength, the investigation has moved rapidly beyond experiment and is well into proof. The rover pair are the perfect delivery system—I utilize testing systems on board to recreate the binary delivery methods outlined in the records we inherited. These are superior organisms, they continue to multiply not only in the track of the vehicles, as I'd intended, but well beyond. I expect great things, and find myself limited by materials and conditions on station. I expect you may solve many of my minor problems.

Point B: I remain your devoted slave at all times.

PI Verita

Averil 07, 407 CSY

From Captain, *Implacable*, to RosaRing Secure COMM 7 for Principal Investigator Only

My Beauty Beyond All, you astound me with your progress, which is prodigious and worthy. You exceed our original goals for so early a date. My progress is less pleasing, our dreams delayed by both orbital mechanics and politics.

Admiral Smit's retirement was received with much division. His ascension to council head was contested and defeated; he demurred taking vice chair. My position is at risk; the opposition demanded the immediate dismantling of *Implacable* as a threat to border peace. This failed, but our military mission has been de-emphasized, and my term on the Fleet Council, which is statutory as *Implacable*'s commander, may end after this voyage.

My crew is far less than full strength. Many retirements and cost-balancings have gone into effect. Review the appended, please. Many experienced officers and crew were replaced by fresh graduates, as if I head a training squad!

Implacable's whole mission is a bargaining point between the parties, as a support ship for the RosaRing. We shall move forward. Your success is paramount to our success.

I am, as always, willing to command such an eager supplicant. Remember that in restriction is liberation.

Captain Kiland

• • • •

THEY had in the course of their bed-talk discussed much that was secret and that stood her in good stead now. The charts, spreadsheets, and projections revealed Kiland as an optimist. Ship's provisioning had suffered. Even a five-year mission was perilous. Weaponry updates were off the budget, savings were achieved by replacing seasoned staff with new graduates, positions left empty, and militia called up for training. Ship's company included too few experienced pilots, and too many untested crew.

Alone in her suite, Verita suffered for Kiland. His setback made her success ever more important. Re-energized by his necessity, she applied herself more fully to duties at hand.

Averil 14, 407 CSY

From Principal Investigator via RosaRing Secure COMM 7 for Captain's Eyes Only

My Strength and Direction, one is desolate to be less than perfect in all things for you. I must request technical aid as well as spiritual solving. So often your lessons bring me clarity.

In the face of Station Admin's orders to conserve fuel can *Implacable* offer assistance until the fuel and drones you carry are delivered? Might a more militant drone-recovery protocol be employed? Can you read signals and plot better courses? Assure me—assure the station!—with your guidance.

I suggest and cannot demand; my Strength reflects yours at all times.

Your latest lesson assists my considerations and will be recalled as often as possible until we are joined again in the harmony of a Perfected Evening.

PI Verita

• • • •

KILAND'S tactical officers enjoyed the challenge of the long-distance scan and solve; they caught the orders as a frolic, as if they were back at school. He had them look for ways to improve the drone's routes, to search for threats in the system, and all threats to the RosaRing. They daily requested more information from the ring. They worked with energy, concentration, amusement.

He was less amused than concerned. The ship's skills depended far more on the practicing of things his staff recalled only from school than they ought.

As captain he deserved a crew capable of supporting his—and the ship's—necessities. Therefore he would push the boundaries of these youngsters. They would become the crew *Implacable* deserved. Each order would be carried out with dedication and devotion. Each solution would be born of submission to the necessity of mission. They would learn. The sub-captain in particular needed growth if he were to serve as a proper second.

Averil 17, 407 CSY

From Captain, *Implacable*, to RosaRing Secure COMM 7 for Principal Investigator Only

Sweet Touch of A Giving Noon, the crew relishes drone tracking. We thank you for the opportunity. The more experienced appear reticent to enjoy our adoption of a Joint Mission. The brightest see that dedication to Mission is all they want.

Your administrator professes surprise at *Implacable*'s ability to compute simple math and solve minor problems in interception. Yes, we can access the telemetry channels of your drones; we pick up signals from your rovers as well. Confederation leaders at many levels lack understanding of what this ship is and what it can do, as they lack an understanding of the RosaRing's potential. We will show them all; we will demonstrate that, together, we can transform planets.

Your administrator embraces details? Perhaps you may offer her more to deal with, so that she may be fully involved in details. She need not be overly concerned with flight planning now that the RosaRing is again in *Implacable*'s shadow.

The tender's co-pilot is a former naval officer; he ought have none of the finicky training the head pilot admires. I append a flight plan for the tender—discussed at mess among the more forward of my sub-officers—which may permit the tender to better retrieve your drones as well as utilize the gravity well to regain lost energy.

I have engaged the co-pilot in a radio correspondence; we discuss a campaign long past in which a ship not unlike the tender was able to overperform simple guidelines designed for ordinary pilots. I, of course, have no orders to give about what must be pilot's choice, nor you; we may simply discuss, suggest, and request.

I remain devoted to the Delicate Delights and such arts you perfect through me, I admonish you to please yourself and please me in all you do.

Captain Kiland

Averil 18, 407 CSY

The pilot's message was not quoted in full; it was apparent that Kiland's suggestions had been acted upon. Alas, the pilot and co-pilot were barely on speaking terms. She? She was unnerved by information that there were now stains on the skin of the tender, where it had driven deeper into the atmosphere than ever before, bringing with it all of the drones. It was a daring mission, no doubt. The pilot had been on sleep shift when the dive sequence began and went to the administrator straight away after they'd returned to the RosaRing. The tender pilot . . .

The tender pilot was not a biologist.

The tender pilot was not a chemist.

The pilot was a pilot. Stains on her ship offended her; and she found them a clear sign that pilot and co-pilot needed a break, each from the other.

There were also stains on the drones, which the pilot cared about not one whit. That was someone else's job. Drones were tended by their own staff, their samples double-checked in the lab.

Verita grimaced. She'd been enjoying a crew amused by the understanding that the *Implacable*'s captain and their own prime investigator were a link-couple. Now she needed to become again the firm scientist and see the entirety of the crew reminded of the necessity for proper isolation technique and contamination control sequences.

Cha-bling, went the annunciator. The administrator's direct line shattered the usual screen image, followed by an image of the administrator herself, chewing her lips, staring at the screen still blank on her end.

Verita composed herself with a deep breath and a straightening of her lab coat; she moved three empty stim cups from screen range. Another centering breath and she was ready to be distantly polite. . . .

"Your comm fails to display, Verita. If you are present, reply so I don't have to send a messenger. This is rather important!"

She composed her expression to what she hoped was a look of general, unalarmed interest, then finished her reach to activate the visual display on her end.

"Important, Administrator?"

"Yes, important! There's an outer-belt asteroid on a collision course with Trikandle. The captain has sent me a secure message! A strike on the planet is within the margin of error, he tells me."

Verita felt her pleasant expression vanish—

"Our mission!"

The administrator offered a grim little smile, apparently pleased with this reaction.

"Yes, our mission, indeed, yes. Also, our station. I gather this 'pass' as he calls it is not immediate but needs be dealt with. There is some factor of resonances and such still being determined. I am not informing the crew, wishing not to spread alarm."

The administrator pursed her lips, her visage taking on the near rictus she assumed when issuing commands not to be denied.

"You shall not tell the crew, do you understand? I *will* direct the captain to inform you of the technical details, and I shall decide what needs be done. I have promised a reply within two shifts, so hold yourself ready for consultation."

With that the screen went back to ordinary.

• • • •

THE CREW took direction well; they'd even taken to the maintenance-plus-pursuit staffing. Given that they were technically shorthanded, with entire Fleet Operations sections of dozens reduced to shifts of pairs, this was a fine way to return the ship to the spit-and-polish days of Smit.

The sub-captain in particular seemed to relish his extra duties. While he'd commanded a small vessel in recent peacetime, his service had not been properly recognized. Passed over several times for political reasons, he, like Kiland, was a volunteer to the *Implacable*. A man with ambition made a good ally.

The sub-captain's shifts responded for him as well as they did for the captain, and he had enough camaraderie with crew to have a mathematician come forward with the threat the asteroid posed several orbits out—which was to say, eleven hundred and seventy-two Standard Years, away. They would chase that asteroid down now. It was the duty of a captain to remove known space hazards.

Reward? The crew would see and taste their own power. For the moment they worked harder and fell into the proper crew-spirit.

Averil 22, 407 CSY

From Principal Investigator via RosaRing Secure COMM 7 for Captain's Eyes Only

My full heart, my hot blood, surely you have outdone yourself! The destruction of that menace delights. It was good that the event could be shared, though some, like the administrator, were shaken by it. In fact, the administrator, speaking confidentially, considers she might order passage on *Implacable* rather than attempt another three years. She asks that I hold updates on my work for the moment.

I have agreed that I could share burden of a Joint Command with her second, and on the other side I have spoken with the Second, who is willing to have promotion sooner. She has been consulting with the physicians to that end.

Admin's oversight of operations has been recently uneven; meals have been late due to minor problems with the energy systems, the air circulators are changed to manual on some shifts as they are affected by a glitch in the attitude controls as we maintain our synchronous orbit above the prime research zone. It is vexing, but to be expected with the staff waiting for decisions easily made. It will be solved soon, I am certain.

On the practical side, the chief tender pilot placed herself on sick leave. The tender's new pilot has been dropping off-the-record radiosondes along with the regular drones. These drop parallel to the rovers; they are wonderfully useful. I see exponential expansion to the limits of the habitat boundaries. We should see blossoming that will change Trikandle sooner rather than later.

My work consumes me nearly as much as my desire to offer myself up to you.

PI Verita

• • • •

THE CAPTAIN was pleased. The crew was brazen in their newfound self-esteem. They'd done something violent and powerful, they'd destroyed—down to gas, plasma, gravel, and powder—a worldlet. The ship might have landed there, the crew might have walked suited in the ravines, collected water from the ice packs. It had been *a place*, and by their action it was gone. They were ready, eager, proven. They searched for more threats, they honed their skills at drills to battle station.

The captain let them strut for themselves; he was willing to admire them, their newfound ambition. They were no longer in awe of the ship—now they were in awe of themselves! Someone had even slipped him a recording of a new song sung on the ship. Made by the same mischievous mathematician who discovered it, the song celebrated *Implacable* and her captain and described the obliteration of the asteroid. The old Fleet might be gone but the urge of youth to bathe in the glory of power had not died!

Averil 24, 407 CSY

From Captain, *Implacable*, to RosaRing Secure COMM 7 for Principal Investigator Only

My Second Heart, I do so desire to share your tremble. Your work engages my crew; we study Trikandle with our sensors and shall share our findings with you. Particularly involved are crew in meteorology and mathematics. I am informed that some regions we'd imaged last trip have changed drastically in these three years. There are streaks of new color evident on the continent you concentrate upon. Also dots of that new color are seen where the rivers flow, around shore lines, ridges, elsewhere. Are the currents and winds so strong? Do the tender flights and the drones work so hard? I shall return to the High Command with evidence of your success.

As always, thoughts of your touch and tone beguile me to sleep; I seek your ministrations.

Captain Kiland

Averil 26, 407 CSY

From Principal Investigator via RosaRing Secure COMM 7 for Captain's Eyes Only

My Partner in Sense and Sensation, I quiver at your approach. The administrator may now opt for very early transfer to *Implacable*, as she is finding sleep and concentration difficult. Several of the lab crew are reporting such issues as well—I ascribe it to general excitement over the approach of your ship.

The changes you report outside the river valleys we've studied amaze. I am not so much sleepless as vibrating with energy and anticipation. I hope the cargo shifts will allow the new drones among the first items available; the old ones have become unreliable. We lost one to weather, an upper current overwhelmed it. A second drone found it crash-landed outside of our prime valley with a large burden of unexpended biotic canisters.

Do tell me you have new challenges and rewards for me, I seek to please you soonest.

PI Verita

Averil 27, 407 CSY

From Captain, *Implacable*, to RosaRing Secure COMM 7 for Principal Investigator Only

Your burden is mine; you will find my requirements a pleasure.

I have requests from your station administrator asking of arrangements for a ceremony of arrival; I hesitate to authorize an on-docking event out of hand. She mentions the possibility of a transfer; paradoxically she requests it and can order it and seems overmatched by her position, indeed. My staff must prompt hers for ordinary transmissions and data sharing; she runs an unprofessional operation, I am afraid.

Can it be that there is a weather wave spreading your new biotics? Is it a chemical reaction catalyzed by the increase in oxygen? Our observers report a surge of color changes on planet; the spectra show unusual mixtures, the temperature sensors show wild variations. Have you science you can share on this?

Supplies will be offloaded by pod and bin; we have become a cargo vessel and are not suited to it! The sub-captain reports basic supplies in the first rounds, and then laboratory items, by necessity of the pod mounts. The pattern is preset.

Do not doubt that I will be firm with you, very soon. I long to hear you whispering.

Captain Kiland

Averil 29, 407 CSY

Glaring at the screen in front of her, Verita rotated the troth ring on her third finger without looking at it. The weight and the repetition were comforting. As much as she twisted it, she couldn't change the fact that docking with *Implacable* was just sixteen hours away, and things were getting worse instead of better.

This latest news from the lab sections was not good. Four of seven biology technicians in the drone research area were on sick call and both of the service mechanics.

She clicked off the message; the staff knew their work. She'd get to them later with a pep talk about yesterday's results. Now, she needed to concentrate . . .

This was not how she'd intended to display a well-controlled station! The mechanics complained of different maladies—one of skin rashes leaving behind a kind of scar, the other of dizziness with headache. All complained of strange odors and odd tastes;

she'd not visited the hangar for days to avoid the sneezes that had become common there. Her own tests . . . well, she was not a medical doctor. It just seemed wise to be cautious and remain in her offices and suite.

It was unfortunate that replacement drones could not be brought to bear sooner. He should have known that chasing the asteroid would add delay . . . but no, nothing about this was *his* fault. Nothing.

• • • •

VERITA opened her eyes, realizing that she'd been swimming in the half-sleep she'd become prone to. A chime in the halls had woken her, one of the administrator's many notes to maintenance.

She was in her own chair, office door locked, so no one saw her start to wakefulness. She was sleeping short shift as she tried to keep up. The returned rovers reported astounding amounts of local free oxygen in the long midafternoon of the planet's forty-hour day. Not an atmosphere breathable by humans, by any means, but one promising explorers might walk the world, extracting the oxygen they needed directly, within a century, perhaps even a decade. She wanted to see it sooner, she wanted to make it happen in a rush of . . .

A chime woke her; the screen was filled by the administrator, her face blotchy and busy with tension.

"Investigator? The tender is under my direct control. Understand me? Until I leave! The pilot's under doctor's care for exhaustion. The backup pilot is nearing the same point. People are ill all around you because you push too hard. You push everyone too hard, Verita."

• • • •

KILAND suppressed the yawn by force of will as he went over routine schedules on the bridge. Smit had always done his paper work on the bridge, too—it was good for the crew to see the leader at work. Lunch was only moments away . . .

"Captain?" The sub-captain's voice was firm. "I don't have any incident reports from the station on this—would you like to take a look on the main screen? I was having some of the crew practice long-range visual ID and we were getting mismatches—"

At high magnification the RosaRing spun in space, filling the screen. The station silhouette was clear but the alternating angled white and blue stripes, clear on large parts of the hull, were smudged and blotchy, as if overlain by a layer of greenish rust around the protruding docking bay on the lower reaches.

"I don't think I've ever seen anything like this, sir."

Kiland's boredom fell away, memory jostling his concentration, trying to come to the front of the mind.

He pointed at a second screen.

"Put some samples from our outbound recorded images there, Sub-Captain, close as you can to a match. Ask Station Operations if they've suffered any gas leakage or maintenance issues they haven't passed on? Get as good an image as you can for them. . . . And ask Ops . . . no, ask the administrator's office to share results of the routine tests they've run on our docking ports and loading locks. Also, request current readings on the inner docks."

"Sir!"

The sub-captain issued commands, brought the bridge to alert, used the keypad to search images and bring them live on screen, ran a match, adjusted sizes.

The ordinary sounds on the bridge fell away; watch partners messaged quick notes or whispered.

The captain hand-signaled the sub-captain, who approached, bowing slightly to hear the captain's order.

Instead, the captain asked, "Were you on academy on the mount, or on the islands?"

The sub-captain, caught by what seemed a non-sequitur, hesitated and said "Why, like you, the islands, sir."

The captain nodded, then nodded toward the images on the main screen.

"So you are familiar with the Citadel's wind walls? Perhaps along Chespick Beach, or the tidal falls at Injridge?"

The sub-captain's features showed remembrance, a touch of a smile for some assignation late night at oceanside, where the waves and wind conspired to produce a lovely romantic place overseen by ancient star-bleached walls smudged at base and higher with the greens, browns, and even reds of algal scums.

Recognition blossomed and . . .

"There's nothing to grow, there's nothing to grow on if there was . . . "

The sub-captain quieted, perplexity wrinkling his youthful visage in much the way passion might.

Kiland nodded and sighed. "Not an oxy world yet, is it? Who knows what's a balmy seaside for what's already growing down there?"

• • • •

"STATION OPS—sir, I'm afraid we woke them up. Our contact is somewhat unfamiliar with standard comm protocols and has 'gone off to find someone' in charge—"

The air quotes were audible.

"—who's apparently dealing with an engineering issue. There seems to be some confusion . . . the administrator hasn't answered a direct call, sir. The automatic transmissions have become sporadic."

"Is anyone talking to us at lower levels?"

The sub-captain queried his consoles.

"Engineering reports they had a contact yesterday, asking for suggestions on dealing with a sluggish stability ring. . . . We sent them updates and a testing program."

Kiland stared at the images, pristine and stained. This could go wrong . . .

"Try again for the administrator and send lunch to my office. If the administrator's office does not respond within five minutes, connect me with the principal investigator. I'm declaring a System Alert; chief pilots should sim-up on irregular rendezvous and docking."

Averil 30, 407 CSY

"Prime Investigator, sir."

Verita heard the connection go through, and looked up. He was handsome, stern. It was good to see him, her own . . .

"Captain Kiland," she said, "I'm informed that the administrator's second is escorting her to the tender, as she is planning to transfer before *Implacable* docks. If both leave this station at the same time, I will be in charge."

There was no privacy, of course—the sub-captain was monitoring the line—so she said no more than the immediate information, waiting for his voice, his support . . .

"We've no flight plan filing on that, Investigator; I'll alert my staff to the potential, though if the stability of the ring is in question they ought not plan on launching."

"There have been some irregularities in the spin, Captain, I think as a result of preparation for docking. There is some issue . . ."

"Are you aware, Investigator, of the buildup on the ring's external surfaces?"

Kiland's face was calm, his voice too neutral to be glad of. Beside his face were video images of the RosaRing looking disreputable, like an out-of-use parts dump.

"I am not—"

"We must have clarity about these stains, Investigator. If they are involved with your stability issues they must surely be solved before we can begin docking. We must have the test results for our docking pilots."

Verita floundered. Her expertise was in living things, not in mundane issues of habitat upkeep. She . . .

"My staff is stretched thin, Captain," she told him, reaching for time to think. . . . "And I am not yet in charge. I will have to study this to . . ."

His expression went bland and she saw him sigh. Then his face went gentle, and she became frightened.

"We cannot enter into final docking procedures until we're sure of the docking mechanisms. Have you access to the records? Surely the dock integrity tests have been done! We cannot query your computer directly without permissions and I cannot risk docking until we have updated information. You must act so that we may properly arrive!"

• • • •

THE SUB-CAPTAIN took the orders without blinking. If the crew blinked, they did so with face bent over screens, following their orders. In a few hours they would be well away from the

RosaRing, orbiting the planet and pacing the station at a distance, any docking approach awaiting developments.

The captain did what a captain does: he let his crew work. It was possible that he could have stepped into any one of the work streams, but they were becoming teams and he would have unbalanced them. The sub-captain directs the crew, the captain directs the sub-captain, and has the big picture.

The tactical crew studied the images; some savant had their computers going over accidental information drawn from the drone reports they'd intercepted. There were more images to be studied for change over time, and possible insight into the stability issues, if engineering could be roused to take a look . . .

Engineering—only a few of the current crew had been on the mission which had brought the station here! Engineering was studying the feasibility of a cold-latch using the very pod mounts they'd used to ferry it here in the first place.

The pod transfer systems. . . . If the standard docking system was compromised, the cargo transshipment would be a logistical terror.

"Captain, Station Ops has someone with experience holding down the deck now, sir. We've got one clear line, and they're asking if we can get some medical advice for them in a hurry. They have a lot of sick people, sir, and she says the administrator's locked in the tender bay, refusing to come out. There's unrest."

Kiland stared into the reflection of deck lights in his troth ring for a half a second.

To the sub-captain: "Add me to the listen list, get a medic online, take any information you can about the physical plant situation. Try to patch through to the line I was on with the principal investigator last shift, open to the command chairs only."

"Sir," was the response, and then he listened.

"And this is?"

The image came from RosaRing's medics; he shared it back across space and waited.

Verita winced when she saw it, her indrawn breath loud between them.

"There is this as well, and this, all isolated within the last hours. Tell me about them!"

Captain to subordinate, the last demand. Verita nodded and began.

"The last image is a fairly common nanopump; it is available for use on restricted crops on many worlds. It biodegrades over time; that one is close to the end of utility. I use them in my work.

"The second image appears to be a blood platelet from an oxygen breather. I'm assuming it is human, and it is malformed—perhaps it has been paired with a nanopump and become separated.

"The first image is an anomaly. We see two of these cell structures, intertwined, one with a cell nucleus being—let us say examined or read—and one with a variant cell in, let us say, production. It uses an alternate chirality to induce evolutionary opportunity."

He said nothing for a moment, shared a list of symptoms . . .

"And this . . ."

"Is not surprising."

"This is native to Trikandle, and it is infecting humans through some strange happenstance?"

Verita glanced at the screen, which made it look to Kiland that she'd been avoiding looking at him.

• • • •

SHE WAS AWAY from the microphone some moments but he heard and said: "It is too late for me to fly by, Verita. We are committed. I must see and report for myself.

"Tell me your exact location. I will find the port closest to you. I will..."

He was under the bulk of the thing, with white and blue and white and blue and white and blue blurring before his eyes to white.... Then blue. He matched velocity until the surface below him barely crawled and then, numbers and letters.

"Forty-four AGAAGF/FE," he said out loud as the gig answered his touch sweetly, approaching hatches auxiliary collars could link to. A hatch outlined, as if sketched over from within, by a collar of red and green crystals around the more prosaic ceramics meant to guard the ship close, even in the no-space that was Jump. His cameras surely transmitted that to the *Implacable*, surely the sub-captain saw the signs...

"Yes," Verita said, "that will be several doors down. I can go there, Kiland."

"There is a wobble," he said, which was true of the ring's motion and not his own.

"The next hatch will provide a better attachment angle. I will check that."

The little vessel let the ring slide on by, and in a moment he heard a sound that might have been a cry or a cough and...

"Kiland, I am not well. It will take me some minutes to get to the next airlock."

"No matter, the time," he said, "*Implacable* awaits my order."

"Yes, but I should move while I can, you see..."

"I have seen what I need to see, Verita. I shall return to the port where you are now. We shall be together very soon."

The gig bumped very slightly against the stain edging the port. "*Implacable*, I am docking. We have blue, blue, blue. Without doubt, we have blue, blue, blue."

"Kiland, tell me where to move?"

"Stay there, Verita. I will come to you. I am solving this."

• • • •

"BEAM BANKS One and Two, go live as leads. The captain has declared a lethal threat situation. We have identified and targeted a threat.

"Prepare to fire on my command, on radar's current target T02. This is not a drill, you will now go to full combat power. Your target should be oversaturated at all wavelengths until plasma. Repeat, until plasma. Await my command."

"Beam Banks Three and Four. Your targets are any rapidly vectoring objects showing planetary escape velocity. Your targets should be oversaturated at all wavelengths until plasma. Repeat, until plasma. Await my command."

"Beam Banks Five through Twenty, your planetary grids are pretargeted and programmed. You will fire until plasma. Repeat, you will fire until plasma. Await my command."

A decisive moment, the image from the gig, showing an empty pilot's seat and board. The forward cams show a fringe of strange color around the docking collar, growing.

"All fire," says the man. "All fire, all fire."

Somewhere, a singer is sobbing quietly at her terminal. The ship trembles. And trembles again, the ship's rotation bringing all the beam projectors to bear, one after another, a rotational broadside searing the ether.

There is silence, and then, loud in the silence of tense breathlessness there is the news of solving:

"Zap."

Dark Secrets

THEY CAME INTO VENZI Station trailing pirates—and riding the redline on a guaranteed delivery, which was far worse.

They were known at Venzi—a scant blessing, so Simon thought, but then, given the current situation, he'd take every small positive thrown their way. At least they'd be allowed to rig to station and maybe even dock, if they could get there.

Caerli was first board, and flying like a madwoman. You'd think it was a gift she'd been given—at least to the point of the pursuit, there being nothing the ex-Scout loved better than to push her own personal piloting envelope.

The nearness of the deadline—neither one of them appreciated that, and it definitely added an extra bit of derring-do to Caerli's flying. His partner had a fond relationship with money. She'd felt the loss of the early delivery bonus keen as if she'd lost a finger. If it came round that they lost the whole fee, it would be a strike to her heart.

Come to it, he wasn't certain in his own mind how they were going to get on, if they lost the payout for this job. Might squeak themselfs into some local work to build the ship's 'count back up to safe levels. That was if there wasn't a fine to pay. Which . . . given Venzi Senior Station Master Tey, there was bound to be a fine to pay.

If they got a fine on top of a loss, Simon thought grimly, they were grounded— plain fact. Despite the station master, Venzi wasn't the worst ring to be grounded on, first reason being there wasn't no actual *ground* . . . but not being cleared to fly—that'd put

45

Caerli 'round the hard bend in local space before a station-day was done, and himself running to keep up.

'Course, he told himself, there wasn't no sense looking so far ahead. Things might work out on their side, yet.

Pirate had range on 'em, after all. Even granting that Caerli could wring miracles from the board, they still might get hull-shredded with no back-up to hand.

And wasn't that a cheering thought.

"We *are not*," snapped Caerli yo'Dira, "going to be hull-shredded."

"Dash every hope I got all at once, why not?" Simon answered, glancing at the screens.

"I'm seeing two missiles with our names on 'em, heading dead on," he said, just giving her the info.

She didn't bother to answer. Thin fingers flew over the board; the screens grayed. Simon's gut insisted that the ship had twisted around them, even as the screens showed real space all about. The instruments reported that they'd Jumped out and in again between one breath and the next.

The pursuing missiles were seventeen seconds further behind them, that being what Caerli's playing of the Ace had bought them, but it was still going to be close—too close, and if—

The universe twisted again, and this time when the screens came back, they were crossing Venzi's shield perimeter. Not the way Jump engines were supposed to be treated, nor the way physics was supposed to be dared. Station warnaways blared across all channels. The missiles, being dumber even than the crack team of Kilsymthe and yo'Dira, didn't answer, and a few heartbeats later the defense system defended the station, just like it was made to do, and there weren't any missiles any more.

The pirates, no surprise, were gone like they'd never been.

"*GelVoken*," came blaring across the all-band. "You will be guided into a Section Eight dock. Lock in and await escort to the station master's office."

The comm light snapped off without waiting for a reply—well. Wasn't any reason to wait for a confirm, was there?

"We were not," Caerli stated, her voice raspy and not quite steady, "hull-shredded."

"That's right," he said, soothing her, 'cause the rush of dancing between life and death pretty often left her shaky. "We didn't get hull-shredded. Good work. I'm thinking Master Tey's gonna give us a citation for that, don't you?"

Caerli all at once collapsed back into her chair.

"Of course," she said. "Whyever else would she send an escort?"

• • • •

"YOU TWO." THE STATION master glared from Simon to Caerli and closed her eyes.

"You two, *again*."

There was that to be said for being known at a particular port or station, Simon admitted to himself – no need to waste a lot of time bringing somebody new up to speed. Station Master Tey, now, she knew exactly who they were.

And she didn't much like them, individually or as a team. Didn't like them *being* a team, for that matter, which happened in more ports than it ought, Terrans and Liadens flying together wan't always a popular choice with admins.

"I guess you had a good and compelling reason for endangering Venzi Station?" Tey asked, sarcasm heavy.

Like they'd deliberately gone looking for a pirate to lead into station, thought Simon with a flicker of irritation. It was understood that a station master had a natural partiality for her station, but that didn't mean the rest of the universe considered it at all interesting.

"We have a commission to Venzi Station," Caerli said softly, reasonably. "We came out of Jump at the Kelestone Light boundary. They were waiting for us, thus we immediately Jumped for Estero— "

That was the story, but she'd short-Jumped there, dropping out well before charted Jump-end to take advantage of one of those asterisked end-notes in the ven'Tura Tables, which always creeped him, and one day Caerli was gonna miss her number and they'd fall outta Jumpspace into the maw of a sun, or the center of a planet. Not that he worried about such things, much.

"We were clear when we came out," Caerli continued, glossing the abort. "Thus, we Jumped for Venzi."

The aborted Jump—that's what'd cost them the early delivery. Still, can't come into a station trailing pirates. Surest way known to pilot-kind to make the station master mad at you.

Case in point.

"You're telling me they were waiting for you at Venzi entry?"

The station master frowned, not liking that notion at all. Which proved she was a good station master, despite the personal lapse of taste that failed to find Kilsymthe and yo'Dira adorable.

Caerli shook her head.

"Station Master, the Jump point was clear. They came in on our tail when we committed to an approach."

Tey liked *that* even less. Pirates lurking along the station approaches was way past serious. Most pirates weren't organized—or numerous—enough to hold a station hostage, though it'd been tried and done. Astrid Verity's Freebooters had held the lanes at Squalme Station for three Standards before TerraTrade hired Canter's Corpsmen to eradicate the problem. Which they'd done, at the cost of near-eradication their ownselves. Mostly, though, your garden-variety pirate didn't have the skill-set—or the attention span—for that kind of long-term commitment.

And, in their particular case, there was an easier culprit, right handy.

"So, your package is interesting to somebody, is it?" asked Station Master Tey. "*Real* interesting, looks like to me."

Simon's stomach fell straight into his boots. He opened his mouth, though their on-going agreement was that Caerli talked to Tey, whenever they could manage it. The gods of lost stars knew what he might've been about to say, but it came moot as Caerli tilted slightly forward, her whole body conveying respect.

"We have guaranteed delivery, Station Master, and the hour fast approaches."

"More fools you, then," snapped Tey.

"Station Master," Caerli adjusted her posture slightly, mixing a smidgen of humble in with the respect. "With all respect, Station Master, if we do not receive the delivery fee, we will be reduced to a cold-pad on station's budget until we may get a rescue from guild or clan."

Simon blinked. It wasn't what either of 'em did, normally, sharing out Kilsymthe and yo'Dira personal bidness with station masters and that sort of person. Nor was Caerli in the habit of admitting she was low on funds.

Then, he saw the calculation behind that startling bit of candor. Station Master Tey saw it, too, and her mouth pursed up like her beer was sour.

Delay the delivery and she'd have Kilsymthe and yo'Dira on her station to deal with every shift until they got lucky—say, forever—or somebody—could be even Tey herself—came to the snapping point and did something maybe, a little, regrettable. Let the delivery meet the deadline, and Kilsymthe and yo'Dira would go away and leave her and her station in peace. More or less.

"All right," she snarled. "Get outta my sight."

Caerli bowed gently, which only made Station Master Tey look more sour.

"Spit it out," she snapped.

"Yes. One only wonders, station master, if we are free to pursue our own business. We had hoped for a speedy departure."

The station master looked at her hard, and Simon could almost see her measuring how much trouble she could still cause them, without being stuck with them forever.

"Make your delivery." There was a pause while she searched the office ceiling with her eyes, and then included them together with a wave of the hand.

"You're on probation and locked to station," she said finally. A glance at both of them, made with a grimace, "It'll be a hot-pad, never fear, but locked to my orders. Admin'll move as fast as practicable, but I want the pair of you where I can find you, in the likely circumstance that questions arise."

Questions about what, she didn't say, and neither of them sought clarity. Instead, in the interest of getting paid, they bowed—and left the station master's office.

• • • •

THEY MADE THE DELIVERY venue—Aberman's Drinkery, which sounded considerably more up-scale than it was—before the wire fell on the deadline, and only that. Caerli went first, with Simon lagging a step behind. His hands, trained for detail and fine work, worried the pay tab.

One long step and he was beside her at the table's edge, packet extended on the palms of his hands, so the man sitting there, scowling, could see it plain.

The *resevio* snorted.

"Took your time," he said, making no move to take possession.

"Yessir," Simon said, "scenic route."

The other man snorted again, and snatched the packet down to the table. He put a hand on it, and glared from Simon to Caerli.

"Will there be a return packet?" Simon asked politely.

"If there is, I can hire me a courier who respects a deadline, an' neither don't take the tab off like it was his to do."

Simon's face heated, but he said nothing.

Caerli bowed slightly.

"If there is nothing more, we depart," she said, and turned on a heel. Simon followed her out into the station hall, and kept to her side as she crossed to a clumsy corner, where two storefronts didn't quite match up, leaving a thin, triangular cubby. At her nod, he slipped into the slim cover first – that was standard operations, him being taller'n her. Caerli snugged in against him, tight and maybe even distracting, save he had a burning question at the front of his mind.

"What're we doing here?"

"Waiting," she answered.

He sighed, and for lack of anything else to do, being squished flat into the corner like he was, he scanned the bit of hall in his line of sight, which included the entrance to Aberman's Drinkery.

It was a back hall, so there wasn't a lot of traffic, though the Drinkery clearly had its adherents. A couple security types strolled in, arm-in-arm, like they was reg'lars, followed pretty soon by a man in mechanic's coveralls, and two women in librarian's robes.

A repair gurney lumbered noisily down the track laid in the center of the hall; three mercs in uniform swung 'round it, walking fast, vanishing before he could read their colors.

The repair rig crawled out of sight, and the hall was empty so far as he could see for the space of four heartbeats.

Three people – two wearing formal jumpsuits, one carrying a lock-case—hove into view. The two formals entered the bar, the third, in full station security rig, shock-stick on her belt, took up position outside the door in one of the classic poses.

"They're never after the *resevio*?" Simon whispered.

"Wait," Caerli said again, which was fine for her, being in front and her backbone not like to meld with a girder.

He hadn't quite become an integral part of the station's structure before the Drinkery's door opened from within, and here came one of the security team who'd gone in prior to the jumpsuits, their own cheery *resevio* walking between him and his partner, one hand cuffed to each. The jumpsuits followed, one still carrying the lock-case. They turned right, the officer who had been guarding the hall falling in behind, passing quite near to the uncomfortable little angle where Kilsymthe and yo'Dira stood concealed. The *resevio's* expression was slack, which was probably due to the pacifier collar laying flat 'round his collarbone.

The little procession passed out of Simon's range, and he sighed out a breath. Caerli stayed where she was, pressing him even tighter into the corner, which he didn't think was possible. He didn't argue her instincts, though, having seen Caerli's instincts at work on numerous occasions in the past.

Finally, she moved, and he did, slowly separating his backbone from the wall. He joined her in the open hallway, and turned with her toward Section Eight docking, *GelVoken*, and some small certain amount of safety.

• • • •

SIMON WENT TO THE BRIDGE, pulling out the pay tab and feeding it to the reader. There was a hesitation long enough for him to suspect that Admin was monitoring their comm, then the green light lit. Accepted and paid. He sighed in pure relief, then headed for the galley.

Caerli'd already drawn two mugs of 'mite and set them on the table. Simon slid into the chair across from her.

"*Resevio's* gonna think we led Admin to him," he said, after he'd had a swallow from his mug. "That's gonna be good for bidness."

"No," said Caerli, and: "The tab?"

"Accepted and paid," he assured her. "'course, speaking of bidness, we pretty much got zero chance to pick up a commission to see us off Venzi. I'd hoped to bolster the treasury a bit."

"No," Caerli said again. "Master Tey wants us off her station. It would also please her if we never returned to her station."

"Ain't *her* station," Simon objected, but his heart wasn't really in it. "Unnerstan, I'm inclined to her mind in this. If I never set foot on Venzi Station again in this lifetime, that'll be fine by me. Oughta at least give it an avoid for the next couple Standards. Let her have time to cool her jets. " He swallowed 'mite. "Or retire."

"That is well so far as it goes—but you are correct that it would be far better if the ship was not forced to fly empty."

Simon shook his head, stood up and carried his empty mug and hers to the washer.

He turned and leaned a hip against the edge of the counter, crossing his arms over his chest.

"Be inneresting to know what we was carrying that pirates was so eager to liberate."

"By now, Station Master Tey will surely have the contents of the packet on her desk. Perhaps she will take your call."

"I'll wait an' read about it in the newsfeed. 'less she calls us in on account of questions having arose."

"That is of course possible," Caerli said politely, her gaze fixed on a point in Jump-space just beyond the edge of the table.

"You don't think they were after the packet," Simon said, with one of the flares of surety that never failed to get him into trouble.

She sighed, and shook her head at that little spot in the void.

"If it was the packet they were after, they would have attempted to board. They fired upon us with earnest intent. Had we not managed to cross into Venzi's space, we risked destruction, and the packet with us."

"They didn't fire 'til last prayers," Simon pointed out. "Coulda been a case o'being certain the packet didn't get to our man at the Drinkery. They'd've rather had the packet off of us, but it'd come down to hard choices."

Caerli moved her shoulders in a fluid Liaden shrug—*yes/no/ maybe*, that meant.

Simon shifted against the counter. Caerli uncertain wasn't what he liked best to see.

"It is . . . too complicated," she said slowly. "If the client needed the packet lost, and herself clearly blameless for its disappearance, there were still less expensive means of arranging the loss. Piracy is a chancy venture with far more risk of failure than success. After all . . ."

Her voice drifted off.

Simon waited until he had counted to one hundred forty-four, then prompted, "After all?"

She started, and looked up at him, her abstraction melting into one of her occasional droll looks.

"After all, we might have won through, and the packet reach the *resevio's* hands."

Simon sighed.

"Screwed up again, have we?"

Caerli shook her head, Terran-wise.

"Had they given us the script, we might have done better for them."

Simon grinned.

"True enough."

His grin faded.

"Caerli."

"Yes."

"They knew where we was going, the pirates."

She sighed.

"So it seems."

"They were *after* us, then, and if not the packet, then—what?" he asked. "*GelVoken*?"

Caerli said nothing, and Simon felt another flicker of surety.

"*Us?*" he said quietly, which wasn't so much of a joke as could be. They'd done some things – not necessarily *wrong*, but not exactly right, neither. For the ship, they said, citing spacer laws of survival, and it'd been true enough. Still, exception could've been took. Revenge might seem to be in order. It was . . . possible—*just* possible—that one of their victims had sworn an affidavit 'gainst them, and offered a bounty.

Bounty hunters, though . . . Simon considered. Bounty hunters were straightforward creatures, who disliked complications just as much as Caerli did. An operation that had them chase a courier through Jump-space—they hadn't, so Simon sincerely believed, ticked off anybody with the means to set a bounty *that* high.

Before they'd become a team—well, he'd traded grey; it was how he'd almost lost *GelVoken* at Tybalt. *Would've* lost 'er, if one Caerli yo'Dira hadn't come by and taken an interest in what was none o'her affair . . .

Caerli . . . Well, he didn't know all Caerli's history, but, after all this time, he knew *her*. She wasn't utterly straight—she loved money too much for that – but she was conservative in the matter of adding new enemies to her string. By listening to what she hadn't said in addition to what she had, he'd arrived at the understanding that her leaving of the Scouts hadn't been her idea; had maybe been in the way of discipline. Still, that'd been close on to ten Standards back; Kilsymthe and yo'Dira having been formed all of seven Standards ago.

"We must do a search of bounties declared and affidavits sworn," Caerli said. "After we have rested."

There was nothing but good sense to that. They were both worn out with adrenaline and long hours at the board.

"Right," he said. "Captain declares all crew on double-down-time, starting immediately."

"Yes," said Caerli, rising. "And if the station master calls?"

Simon looked black.

"Station master calls, she can leave a message."

• • • •

SIMON'S DOOR WAS STILL closed when Caerli ghosted down the hall to the galley, some few hours later. She, who had training that Simon did not, had accessed the so-called Rainbow technique to insure a deep, healing sleep, rising refreshed and focused in under a quarter of a shift. Simon would sleep yet for several hours. Adrenaline burned through his reserves quickly; the strain of the pursuit had already exhausted him, before they came to the necessity of coping with Station Master Tey and her little intrigues.

Caerli carried a cup of tea and a protein cookie with her onto the bridge, and settled into the co-pilot's chair, as was proper. *GelVoken* was Simon's ship, after all, however much he might credit her with returning it to him. They were operating partners, but not co-owners.

Perhaps she ought not to have accepted his offer of a partnership, but she determined that she was going to reform, to leave her previous life, and start afresh. It had seemed she was owed that, were Balance the natural state of the universe—the ideal on which the whole of Liaden civilization was predicated.

She had been desperate, she thought; certainly, she had not been naive. Even then, she had known that the natural state of the universe was chaos.

Even then, she had known that one could not outrun the past, no matter how able a pilot one was.

She slowly ate her cookie, considering how best to proceed.

Easiest for all, if An Dol contacted her. Sadly, An Dol had liked to play games, and if she was tempted to think that had changed over the years, she had only to remember two missiles in the screens, dead on and gaining. It was barely possible they were live with no warhead, to prove a point. Exactly what he might have done, before, except the last time they'd met, he had sworn he was through playing games.

The last of the protein cookie went in a crunch as she considered the likelihood of that.

No, An Dol still played games.

That being so, he would expect *her* to find *him*.

Caerli sighed and drank her tea. Truly, she was in no mood for games, nor in being forced back into An Dol's service—which, belatedly, made her wonder what it was he wanted her *for*. He had ruined her as a Scout, seen her discharged without honor, so she was no use to him in the old way. She had rebelled when he would use her as a drudge—and for years, he had . . . one might say *allowed* her . . . to remain at liberty.

That he came looking for her now . . . there must be something new afoot; something for which her skill-set was uniquely fitted.

Well. There was an unsettling thought.

She closed her eyes and partook of the benefits of another calming exercise.

Whatever An Dol wanted, it was imperative that he be kept away from Simon.

Simon possessed a varied set of skills and strengths, peculiar to a man who had split his young life between space and bronk-herding. His grey-trading had root in the habits of his planetside father and uncle. Simon could track a bronk on hard high plains, kill a witchbird with his bare hands, and skin a chardog with his belt knife—or so he claimed. Whether or not these particular claims were true – and she did not see why they should not be—Simon's abilities were impressive, and occasionally startling. What he did not have was a true appreciation of the subtlety a high-born rogue Liaden might employ to grasp power, or to expand it.

Which meant that her counter was inside An Dol's orbit. Little as she relished it, she would need to go onto Venzi Station, and play seek-and-be-stealthy with An Dol.

Before she allowed misdeeds and *melant'i* of the past to claim her, however, she would embrace one more opportunity to act with honor.

She leaned to the board. A series of quick finger taps on the board opened her personal files. Another hundred faultless keystrokes and she had done all that was needful. She purged the files, sat back in her chair, and reviewed her options.

Truth, she thought; she had none.

Best, then, to get on with it.

She rose, placed her ship-key on the board where Simon would be certain to see it, and left the bridge, mug in hand.

The mug, she left in the washer in the galley before proceeding down the hall to her quarters, where she armed herself, and shrugged into her Jump-pilot's jacket.

Thus armored against An Dol's sense of play, she left *GelVoken* by the service hatch, and made certain it sealed behind her.

• • • •

CAERLI WAS UP BEFORE him, which neither exceeded his expectations, nor hurt his feelings. Simon stopped in the galley to draw a mug o'mite, and moved down to the bridge, which was where he'd find her, certain enough. A thought had come to him while he'd been drifting up toward wakefulness. Might be they could check for small cargo on the salvage and surplus side. *GelVoken* could take a mini-pod; didn't often 'cause neither him nor Caerli was a born trader, but the option was there. An' if they were just hauling to another yard of like character, there wasn't no trading involved. Flat fee and not likely to be much of it, but ship's bank was low enough he'd—

The bridge was empty.

Simon blinked, and for no reason at all his stomach clenched. So, Caerli was still resting—or resting again. No reg against that, was—

It was then that he saw the ship key in the share tray between the two boards, and the message light blinking yellow.

He stepped up to the board, accepted the message with a touch, and stood looking down at a short list of files and account codes, balances appended, which was Caerli's private money, every one of 'em bearing his name as 'counts holder. At the end of that list was a note, cold as if they'd been strangers, traveling together by chance.

Captain Kilsymthe. I resign my berth, effective immediately. Caerli yo'Dira, Pilot.

He was shivering. He noted the fact like he was reading it off the screens. His fingers moved, bringing up the call log, finding it empty.

Just gone for a ramble out on the station, then. She did that. Done it many times.

Hadn't ever before found it necessary to leave her ship-key behind her, or roll every single bit of her private money over to him. Not to mention leaving resignation letters just a little bit colder'n deep space.

Simon closed his eyes.

Something bad was happening, that was what. And before it got any worse, he had to find Caerli.

• • • •

IT WAS . . . UNSETTLING, how easily the rules of An Dol's play came back to her. He had cast her as the supplicant, the seeker; *the lesser*, to whom he would reveal himself in the fullness of time and grant her succor—it would be succor, for An Dol played with live weapons. Had she not successfully eluded his missiles, An Dol would have seen that her abilities had atrophied, and that it would have been an error to trust any longer in her survival skills.

That she had played her second Ace, ensuring the survival of *GelVoken*, Simon, and herself proved that she was still worthy of him—and now the game went to a higher level. She could expect ambushes and assassins before An Dol revealed himself to her.

Best, if she found him before he was ready to step forward. It would annoy him, and An Dol made mistakes when he was annoyed.

She paused in the shadow of a cargo hauler, surveying the dockside and considering where he might be.

One might think he could be anywhere, and Venzi Station large enough for a man who wished it, to stay hidden for years.

Only, An Dol did not wish to be hidden; he merely wished not to be found until he had made his point and had his fill of fun.

So, then, he would be near *GelVoken's* docking, but not in Section Eight itself. Not that An Dol wasn't bold enough to secret himself on the station master's own dockside, merely that, for this game, it would not suit his purpose.

For it must be assumed that his purpose, in part, was to remind her, forcibly, that she was his inferior. He would see her hurt before he stepped forward to rescue her from worse.

Dockside would certainly suit him, much more than the civilized, and patrolled, core rings. A certain *sort* of dockside, certainly; the station's equivalent of a lawless zone—a low port—The Ballast, so it was referred to on Venzi Station.

Assuredly, An Dol would bide his time, awaiting her in The Ballast.

• • • •

SIMON PAUSED AT THE edge of their docking area, looking around, for a hint, a clue —for Caerli walking down-dock toward him, arms 'round the waists of a brace o'port dollies.

Woman didn't leave her life's blood to her partner because she was gonna surprise him with a party, he told himself, and looked around some more.

Caerli was cautious; she was stealthy, and if she didn't wanna be found, well— there was a one in a million chance that the likes of Simon Kilsymthe would find her. On the other hand, one in a million was still odds. He wasn't beat yet.

He found the place where she'd paused for a bit, thinking out her next move, maybe. And he found that one heel—her left—had rested in a bit of drink-smudge, so that when she took her first step onto the public way, a sticky little crescent was pressed to the decking, and there, just at the proper length for Caerli's short, determined stride, was another, and beyond that one, a third . . .

The crescents faded finally, but by then, he had a direction, sensing rather than seeing where her feet had tred, and he hurried on.

Damn it, if Caerli had it in mind to take on The Ballast by way of letting off a little steam, he surely wanted to be in on the fun.

• • • •

SHE'D NULLIFIED TWO attackers on her way across The Ballast, and frightened off a third. It was unfortunate that the second of her two attackers had some skill as a knife-fighter. He had touched her, and though she had wrapped it, she became aware of shadows gathering in her wake as she moved toward her goal; the honest citizens of The Ballast, that was who followed her now, scenting blood, and easy prey.

She kept her attention forward, seemingly oblivious, until one of her hangers-on took the bait, and darted forward, making a feint toward her pocket.

She spun, knife out. The would-be pickpocket raised her hands and backed away.

"Peace, now, Pilot. Cain't lay blame for a fair attempt."

"Your next attempt will be your last," Caerli said, matter-of-fact, and making sure her voice carried to the others, waiting at some distance. "I'm on business and I will not be interrupted."

"Certain, Pilot, certain. Ana fine shift to ya."

The pickpocket faded back into the pack of watchers; the watchers thinned away and were, to eyes less sharp than Caerli's, gone . . .

She turned and continued on her way. Not long now, by her estimation.

• • • •

THE BALLAST OCCUPIED a trapezoid section of less-than-premium space between the back-up power coils and the emergency gyros. The door you wanted from Section Eight Docking was near the narrow end of the section; which was mostly transfer slots, and grab-a-bites, and fun houses. Simon did a quick tour of the possibles, put a couple of questions, and found Caerli not at all.

Onward, then, he thought, into the deep and dangerous side. He sighed. He wished he'd known Caerli'd been in this tone o'mind; hadn't seemed to be the case when they'd parted company, each to get their own rest. 'Course, Caerli was private— and there was still the question of her putting all her most valuables under his name. Sure, The Ballast was rough, but it wasn't anything like Caerli to consider she wouldn't survive a little bit o'exercise 'mong the station-bound.

• • • •

IT WAS NOTHING MORE than a hunch that turned her steps toward the repair hall. At the last, it always came down to hunches, with An Dol. If she was right, she'd soon enough have confirmation.

She was right.

They came boiling out of the dark storefronts ahead of her, and more, from the cross-corridor she had just passed. Others came out of the deep shadows at the side walls. A melding, Caerli saw, as she spun lazily on one heel, taking in the fullness of them. A dozen—fifteen, perhaps—the five in spacer's motley putting themselves forward, letting her see their faces. Of them, she thought she recognized the woman whose bald head was tattooed with a world's wonder of flowers, and possibly the man with the silver sash round his ample middle. The other three spacers were strangers: the rest of the mob were Ballasters, hugging the shadows, holding weapons that at other times were slotdrivers, span-hammers, and punch-blades.

Fifteen, five trained in An Dol's particular school of survival.

It occurred to her that An Dol wanted her dead, after all; that he had drawn her to him so that he might witness her ending in person.

Well. Fifteen against one, was it? From An Dol's perspective, it might be a compliment.

The least she could do was to show her appreciation.

She kicked, diving for the floor, hitting with her left shoulder and rolling.

One of her throwing knives found a nesting place in the breast of the tattooed woman; the second in the eye of a Ballaster who had darted in, hammer raised. Her gun was in her hand, and she managed three quick shots into the crowd before she was engulfed and it was fists, and feet, and knives.

• • • •

IT WAS THE SHOUTING that drew him into a run. One sight of the melee and he knew it could only be Caerli in the middle of it all. There were bodies on the decking here and there—dead, or nearly so, silent acks to his notion that this was no ordinary rumble, but Caerli fighting for her life, no regard for grace.

And expecting to lose.

Never in the all the long years they'd been together had he known Caerli yo'Dira fighting to lose. Woman fought the odds like they was personal, and he'd long ago lost count of the times she won over them, by willpower and cussedness.

Simon paused on the edge of the bidness, taking stock, testing the angles, wondering if it were better to start shooting, hoping they'd scatter, or—

"Why, what have we here?" A voice murmured in his ear. "This is most unexpected."

Simon spun, gun out and right in the face of a Liaden man dressed neatly in leathers, and a wide, Terran-style grin on his face.

"It is the partner, is it not?" he said, paying so little attention to Simon's gun that he had a moment's belief that there was no gun in his hand at all.

"Simon Kilsymthe," he growled, and jerked his head toward the melee. "If you can call that off, do it."

"I can," the Liaden said, his brows pulling slightly together. "The question, I believe, is—will I? And, do you know, I think I might. For considerations."

"What considerations?"

"Surrender your gun and yourself to me, now."

"And I'd do that—why?"

"Because if you do not, Jezzi, who stands behind you, will take your gun, and I will allow nature to take its course with respect to your partner, and my former associate."

Simon risked a glance to the side, catching a glimpse of Caerli. She looked bad, and if she got out of this mess alive, she'd flay him for doing what he was about to do. He looked forward to that, but in the meantime, this being a Liaden he was dealing with, he had to secure both sides of the promise.

"I give you my gun, you'll call off the fight," he said.

"I will call off the fight, if you give me your gun. That is correct."

Simon reversed the gun and extended it, butt front.

A hand snaked over his shoulder and took possession. The Liaden stepped away from Simon. Simon turned to face the riot.

From his belt, the Liaden withdrew a flare gun. He pointed it to the girders above, and fired.

Sparks filled the hallway, riding an ear-punishing *boom*.

"Freeze or fall!" a voice shouted, over the echoes. "Freeze or fall!"

The sound of safeties being snapped off numerous pellet guns was almost as loud as the boom.

In the center hallway, the melee sorted itself into some kind of order. Those who could rose, some leaning on the nearest shoulder. As if obeying some unheard command, they pulled away from the battered figure, bent and kneeling. She was panting, and there was blood on her face; her left arm hanging bad.

Slowly, she raised her head, and Simon saw her recognize the Liaden with a grim resignation he'd never before seen on Caerli's face.

"So, An Dol," she called, her voice hoarse. "Will you finish it yourself?"

"That had been the original plan," the Liaden—An Dol—said, cheerfully matter of fact. "But someone has entered a side bet, and thus made the game more diverting. You have a reprieve, Captain yo'Dira. Your partner stakes his life for yours."

Simon saw her blink; she moved her head carefully, and her eyes met his.

"Simon," she said. "You idiot."

• • • •

"YOU WILL SCARCELY CREDIT it, I know, Captain Kilsymthe," the Liaden named An Dol said chattily, "but our so-dear Captain yo'Dira had been an associate of mine."

He wanted Simon to ask him for details, but Simon was smarter than that, at least. He said nothing, and hoped he managed to look a little bored.

Before the silence stretched too long, An Dol continued, not seeming to mind Simon's lack of curiosity.

"She was a Scout, you know, working for the Archivist's office. Her duty was to gather Old Tech and either destroy it, or tag it for retrieval and destruction. Sadly, she found herself in want of cash, so she sold a piece—quite an insignificant piece—to one of my agents. Well, you know how it is with honor, do you not, Captain Kilsymthe? Once broken, never mended. It was easier the second time, and even easier the third. By the fourth sale, I don't believe she even needed the money, and by the time the Scouts discovered her breach and discharged her, finding Old Tech for me was second nature to her. She was for a time among my crew; she really is very skilled at finding the caches of old machines, and is an able technician, besides. Matters proceeded in an orderly fashion, satisfactory to all for a number of Standards.

"Then, there was a mishap—perhaps a Scout was killed. It may, in fact, have been a team of Scouts. Regrettable, but it seems Captain yo'Dira knew them, and did not agree with my necessity. She left me soon after, and I—I let her go, because I knew I could find her again, should I ever want to do so."

Caerli was sitting on a stool next to Simon. She'd been patched up, rough, with a first aid kit. She hadn't said a word since greeting her partner. If he didn't know better, he'd've said she was asleep.

Now, she raised her head.

"What do you want, An Dol? If you've decided to kill me, do it, and let Pilot Kilsymthe return to his life."

An Dol laughed.

"You have undoubtedly taken several blows to the head, so I will not berate you for stupidity. How shall I let Pilot Kilsymthe go, when he has seen me, and will shortly know of my workings? Indeed, the more I consider this new situation, the more I like it. The two of you are known on Venzi as troublemakers. It will make the scenario more believable, if both of you are in it together."

"What scenario?" asked Simon, to save Caerli the trouble.

"Why the scenario where Captain yo'Dira smuggled a disrupter onto Venzi station, and she and her partner, after contacting the station master with demands, and being, as I imagine they will be, rebuffed, decide to demonstrate the strength of their position. Which they will do—sadly forgetting to take themselves to a place of safety beforehand."

He paused, frowning slightly.

"What is the Terran phrase? Ah. Screw-ups to the last."

Simon was opening his mouth to ask what a disrupter was, but Caerli's raw voice cut him off.

"You're going to disrupt a section of this ring? Which section?"

An Dol smiled, and it came to Simon right about then that the man wasn't sane.

"Why, I think The Ballast will do nicely, don't you? We shall demonstrate, and rid Venzi of a trouble spot, all in one throw. Balance shall be maintained."

"And then?" demanded Caerli.

"Then? Why we shall perhaps need to stage a second demonstration; we are prepared to do so. I am determined to have this station. We need a base from which to operate, and there are several like-minded teams who would join us here."

Simon's stomach was not happy. Crazy or not, An Dol had ambition. *This* pirate wasn't just going to occupy station *space*, he was going to occupy *the station*.

He looked at Caerli, hoping to see some sign that she thought An Dol's little scheme was doomed to fail.

He saw the exact opposite.

• • • •

IT WAS AN ELEGANT LITTLE machine, Simon thought, hardly any bigger than his head, and at that seeming too small to catastrophically shut down all systems in The Ballast.

Be a bad death, too, which Simon wasn't looking forward to.

"Now," said An Dol. "Captain yo'Dira, you will call the station master and deliver your lines. In the event that you should consider an ad lib, I offer you this."

The gun was buried nose-deep in Simon's side, and An Dol was behind him. If Caerli deviated, he'd be gut-shot, which would, Simon couldn't help noting, be a quicker, cleaner death than the rest of The Ballast was going to get. Caerli being Caerli, she might well think herself entitled to make that choice for him. Which, being honest, and their places switched, he might think the same.

Caerli gave him a long, unreadable stare, then turned to the comm screen and fed in the station master's call-code.

"You!" Station Master Tey growled. "Where are you? I been trying to find you the last half-shift."

"I have been busy, Station Master. Forgive me if we have presented an inconvenience to you."

"An inconvenience? You might say that. Do you know what was in that packet you brought onto my station?"

Caerli tipped her head slightly to the left.

"An Old Tech tile rack," she said.

Tey took a hard breath.

"You knew that, and you still brought it here?"

"I did not know when we accepted the commission. I have only belatedly deduced what it must have been."

"And you're calling me because of your powers of deduction?"

"No, Station Master." Caerli took a deep breath, and Simon sighed out the one he'd been holding. "I am calling to report an emergency situation."

The phrasing, that's what gave An Dol a distraction, a hesitation in his eyes—just the smallest possible hesitation, but that was all Simon needed. He sidestepped, ducked, and swung, knocking the gun arm high, belt-knife leaping to his other hand.

One strike, straight to the heart, just like he was putting down a rogue bronk.

The dying fingers tightened on the trigger; the gun discharged; and Caerli leaned into the screen, speaking rapidly.

"Station Master, Venzi has been invaded by pirates, and is in mortal danger. You must immediately dispatch security teams to all sensitive controls. You are looking for devices—possibly Old Tech, possibly of modern make—set to disrupt critical station systems. We are in The Ballast with one such Old Tech machine. I am going to attempt to defuse it. If I fail, Venzi will lose this section."

Station Master Tey was staring.

"What ship?" she asked.

"*Chandivel*, out of Liad. Station Master, time is possibly short."

"Yes. Get to work, Pilot."

The screen went blank, and Caerli spun toward the device, stepping over An Dol's dead body.

"Well done, Simon," she said briskly. "Please access The Ballast's internal comm and announce an evacuation."

• • • •

WELL, THERE WAS BOUNTY money, which came to them, and left over a tidy sum, even after the fines had been deducted—the fine for bringing Old Tech onto Venzi, and the other one, for bringing pirates.

There was salvage, too, one-twelfth of the value of *Chandivel*, which plumped up the ship's account to levels last seen by Simon when he was a boy and his ma *GelVoken's* captain.

Simon had reversed Caerli's gifts, of course, and made her a third-part owner of *GelVoken*, even before all the funds were in. Someone that invested in him and his deserved a little for herself, too.

Also, they was free to go, with an invite from Station Master Tey not to visit again soon, which they promised, best they could.

"Comes to me," Simon said, when they was on their way to Venzi Jump-point, "I never did thank you for nearly getting me gut-shot."

"Co-pilot's duty," Caerli said, which was true enough.

"You got any other dark secrets in your past likely to come 'round and make us into targets?" he asked.

There was a small silence, and he looked over to find Caerli watching her screens with a fair degree of concentration.

"In fact, I am made clanless for my indiscretions," she said, quietly. "That need not concern you. There is nothing else, except—you know, Simon, the usual sort of thing."

Right.

"Well," said Simon; "just so long as that's clear."

Revolutionists

"ARIN'S ENVIDARIA, *as instituted for the Seventeen Worlds by Arin Gobelyn's son Jethri Gobelyn and overseen by the Carresens-Denobli, established an egalitarian trade network meant to be self-supporting during the disruptive incursion of Rostov's Dust into the lesser galactic sub-arm.*

"Jethri Gobelyn, a peripatetic traveler and trader, left his mark in many ways; his genes are said to be widely dispersed in and around the Seventeen World trading nexus. Due to divergent local institutional traditions the Seventeen Worlds Network experienced a period of instability following the end of the dust-dark and the reestablishment of regular trading with the wider Terran-Liaden trading web."

—Gehrling's *Middle History of the Inhabited Galactic Sub-Plane,Third Terran edition*

Geral was alone, as he often was. This time was different because he was doing squad work solo instead of with the whole squad. Famy Binwa'd called him sudden.

"We got a big meeting for only Full Staff and Seniors, no cits allowed. Secret, too, you can't mention it. You're covering for Security. Get to it!"

Another drill, he'd figured, but once his ID read as present in Service Squad's corridor, Binwa'd said, "Not a drill this time, Geral. You're mobile structure security! Watch yourself, there's been trouble!"

So he went careful. The logs did show trouble—odd trouble. Bar fights gone to flash-riots, followed by attempts to enter Admin without permission. Sabotaged cameras. Yeah, the cits weren't pleased with Admin changing anything—heck, people would argue and fight if their old veeds disappeared and no chance to stuff 'em into personal holdings, much less work shortages and menus gone thin.

Down here in the inner structure, though, he ought to be fine, no real chance of riot or change to threaten him. Binwa'd sounded tense, like Geral might not be up to the job.

It didn't help Geral that he'd been raised like he was fragile, him being a good birth in a bad Standard Year. In fact, him and Luchee being the only pair born across three hundred and ten days—and before-hand some doubts he'd be born at all.

Once he *was* born they were careful of him—after him there were three years in a row with no births, period. They said it was the famine that did it, but then the cheese planets got back in gear after their little civil war and things got back to regular. Kids was born station-side again—they used fertility drugs and had a bunch of twins and triplets—so there were always a pack of youngers that he didn't quite fit in with.

The Seniors, it was known, kept him in reserve as a special case, 'cause he had good blood, since it was the 'fusions that let them get to their proper ages and the 'fusions that kept them safe during the thin-food. They'd been so close-knit that cousins were sisters and little brothers nephews. They tested him and never tapped him, but they kept his mother close. She had the blood and had survived his birth sturdy, even in those bad times.

His mother—he hadn't seen her for almost a Standard Year; she'd gone up deck and was living in Senior Pod, where the Seniors had their own medico and kept their own shifts. The last time he'd seen her, he'd been on 'cide clean-up. She'd been in a hurry elsewhere and had stopped when she saw him, nodding a greeting.

"Looking good, Geral Jethri. Don't join no rowdies, and don't think you need a way out," here she'd gestured to the 'cide site, "'cause you're set. I'm good for years and you—you're in the right orbit. You got the blood, so they'll hold on to you like they hold on to me. The Seniors need you! I'll see you about, I bet."

That orbit had brought him here, after all, with him having not spoken to her again.

He patted the metal turnwheel at the master seal between open corridors and the utility tunnels. He tested the seal with a gas sniffer. He looked for little hidden messages. His comm unit was on channel, so he spoke to it.

"Seal three checks out, Binwa, got the veed. No hosties, no notes."

No reply for the moment, but Famy Binwa was always a tad slow in the Control room, more afraid of making a mistake than—

Mud, ought to use the correct form, shouldn't he? Things were spelled out proper on Security Detail, especially for Binwa, who was a boss because his ma was and not so much 'cause he knew what he was doing.

Silence went on. Binwa got touchy, but not like he was a bad sort—they'd talked many times about how things might change now that the curl of the dust the system'd been stuck in for three hundred Standards was drifting out. Lately Binwa was always on duty when Geral was, like they were going to be paired on the low shift forever, like kids being left to deal while the adults did something for adults.

"Please repeat, Squad," Binwa finally insisted.

Geral translated this time, from the start, his voice sounding odd in his own ears, which meant Binwa'd just turned the recorders on and his mic was live.

"Attention Internal Control. Squad Forty Security Update. Seal Three is tight. No hostiles. No anomalies."

"Squad Forty, we confirm your voice match, we confirm your location, we confirm no hostiles, we confirm Seal Three is secure, we confirm there are no service reminder notes. Please move to next station. Veed feed as time permits."

He hadn't found any hostiles so far. Hostiles in his early training had always meant Yxtrang invaders, but that was a scare tactic to help kids keep serious. His whole life, born and bred here, he'd never heard of an actual Yxtrang station invasion. So far as he'd ever seen, a hostie was a Security full-timer slurping toot or half asleep over a streaming 'venture veed.

These days the threat was supposed to be Revolutionists, a secret group trying to change the way things on Spadoni Station worked and who was in charge. He'd never met any of them outright, though some of the tougher hanger-abouts might could be. They'd complain that things needed changing—that it used to be you was free to work at what you wanted or what you could, but now they were being sent to the cheese planets on contract, want to or no! Somehow it was Admin doing things wrong, or the Seniors who needed replacing to make things right.

The Revolutionist talk had gained a lot of energy in the last quarter, what with Odd Things happening Out There. Out There being other sectors, sectors they were hearing more and more about because the dust was thinning so rapidly. Outside hadn't been important growing up, except that it made the Seventeen Worlds allies because of the *Envidaria*.

He'd read the *Envidaria* a bunch of times, and you could say he believed in it. To stop one world being the top spot like Liad tried to do, the *Envidaria*'d kept the sides even . . . and that meant worlds shouldn't own all the ships, all the stations, all the commerce. Spadoni was 'sposed to be independent, her people free to work at what they could, while the trade org belonged to the planet system and most of the ships came from Outside. The *Envidaria* was supposed to make that work.

He'd also read a bunch of the couldies about *Envidaria*, the idea. They were made-up things like *The Secret of Lord Jethri*, *The Clouds of Spite*, and yes, even a buncha the mances like *Three on A Ship* and *The Master Firegemster*. It was kind of funny seeing the images of Jethri on this very same station back when it was fresh-built, and knowing he, Geral, carried part of that name, and that he really did, if you squinted, look like Jethri. Stars in his blood, courtesy of his multi-great-grandma's bunking with the man with the plan.

• • • •

GERAL LINGERED in Corridor Nine, feeling a little homesick.

He'd brought Luchee to the 9-9 storeroom for a kiss and some touches back when he was just Deck Plus, and even showed her Vent 77, the inactive space that was technically just a Three Seal since it had been a part of the temporary build-in docks meant for short term storage. Him and Luchee'd been of an age, and 'bout as poor, both born to mothers on station base pay. The mothers lived cubbywall to cubbywall, shared corridor frontspace, and on slowdown weeks they sat out front with everyone else, passing sips while the kids hunted stuff to turn in for credits at the recycle, being too young to trade blood for points. Once he'd been born and was proof her line was clean, that was the start, and after he hit puberty they knew he didn't break his bones just by standing, or bleed forever, nor any of the other problems that had come along to stationers in the rough times a couple hundred Standards goneby.

Him and Luchee, they'd got in a fight once, a fierce thing where they wasted some of that precious blood arguing about if it was *good* to trade blood in.

"Points are good and you know it. Have to save a little extra," he'd told her.

She'd squinched her face up, looked those grey eyes straight at him. "You do it more than once and it'll go on your records. And then you'll get stuck, just like your ma. She can't go higher, 'cause Admin keeps her like she's a crop down in 'ponics!

"I see my own ma just waiting for the points to rack up and I'm not gonna live like that and neither should you.

"I could just shake you sometimes for not paying attention!"

Well, she did shake him, and he shook her back, and somehow they hit a gravity well frustrated with each other. And there was the blood, and needing to clean it up before someone called a safety on them for creating a hazmat situation.

In the end they'd patched it up and kept hanging together. They promised each other they'd keep their blood and use all that extra energy to study. They even did some joint Informatics until their skills didn't match any more. Luchee was good with maths, and she'd been set to student status, 'cept all the classes were always full of the C and B deck folks and no room for her, no matter how high her test scores were.

Him, the one Luchee was always getting out of scrapes—*he'd* been free to study how he wanted—station stuff, and the *Envidaria*—always interested as much in how the station worked as in how far he could go updecks in life. So, turned out, *he* could make a living doing what he wanted, and *she* couldn't even go to school, nor get anything better than hour-work.

Luchee and him had thrilled a couple times in the vent space in Corridor Nine but he gave it up after he'd stopped by to find her there not very dressed and with an older guy from up Admin Deck just as sweaty and calling her name like he was hurting, which still made him twitch to think about even if it was a few years back.

She might have warned him, anyhow . . . but she hadn't, and they'd got all disconnected over it, with her saying things was too complicated for her to talk about with him anymore, and levels he had no business to know—him being in the Service Squad and his ma still transfusing.

She wouldn't know him, then, and he got busy with his doin's, so he forgot to miss her, 'til he heard she'd connected with a visiting spacer, and gone off as side-crew with no notice to no one. He figured that was luck for her and he did miss her, though by then he had a crew-grade sleep-unit, and didn't need the cubby, anyway.

"Squad Forty, this is Green Office." Binwa's voice in his ear jerked him out from remembering. "We have inbound ships and I have to check-mark all the security stations. No one's covering the armory. I have keyed your unit in; I need you to go there and sit at the boards, it's supposed to be occupied when ships approach."

"Green Office, Squad Forty is just one of me, and that's supposed to be a three-crew location, according to training. I . . ."

"*This* is also a three-crew location and there's one of me, Squad Forty. We are in security lockdown mode because of that meeting. Go, lock yourself in, report. The hatch is set to your ID."

"I'm on my way. Does route matter?"

"Squad Forty . . . call it a hurry, and I don't care how you get there long's you do it quick."

"Confirmed, this is a hurry and I'm on free route. Going."

• • • •

THE ARMORY had opened to him, as Binwa'd told him it would. Geral rushed into the control area and was in front of the screen, helmet and gloves off, still sweating—and only part of that from the path he'd followed. He looked at the controls, familiar only from sim, and worried, thought of Luchee getting stuff right off and figured he could remember what he had to here.

He was trying to get his balance back on account of the tween-deck utility shafts he'd run as fast as he could. The places where you could be caught in gravity errors where you got pulled in two or three directions from overlapping grav fields or where weak fields might let you dive down a metal tunnel for meters on end.

"Squad Forty! Check that hatch!"

Geral twisted his head.

"Closed." It had made a muffled thrum when he'd pushed it across hard.

"Not showing good here!"

He rose carefully, left leg and knee a trifle sore from a missed gravity slip. It hadn't been there last time he was through . . . but that happened these days as the fabric of the station strained against its age. It should have been refitted before he was born, but there'd been the Troubles, after all.

He twisted the handle and slid the hatch open an arm's length. He hadn't tested the pressure gauges and now his helmet sat at the second seat, with all his readouts . . .

He pulled, sullenly, and yelled across the room as it slammed . .
.

"Now?" He forgot his formal again, but then so did Binwa, who was sounding strained.

"Not sealed!"

Geral pulled his weight against the handle, yanked it open, staring into the hatch mechanicals.

"Mud and wind twists!"

There were four pressure latches meant to grab and seat when the handle was rotated. One close to his hip level was fine and bright, and the one just above chest height was, too. The top and bottom latches though, looked like they had something in the way of that final click-seal, something printed in a very thin flex-sheet that fell into place after the hatch was cycled once.

"What was that, Squad Forty?" Now Binwa sounded *really* worried.

Fingers quick on the sharp metal hatch edge, Geral pulled hard, and out came the bottom strip, unfolding to near half his arm length. He stared, shoved it into a storage pocket on the duty-suit, reached to pull the other while . . .

"Problem spot, *hold comm*," he managed, and emphasizing that helped him pull the tattered top strip down to shove it, too, into his pocket.

"Jonimo!" He slammed the hatch hard, and this time the click sounded like a solid thunk, all right, and . . .

"Jonimo?" came the worried voice and then: "That's got it!"

He sat heavily at the console, pulling a frayed yellow strip from his suit.

"Is that code, Squad Forty?"

Geral gasped a short laugh, wiping sweat from his forehead.

"Kind of is, Binwa. Haven't you ever done a suit-walk? *Jonimo* is what you say when you jump off the station, to tell your squad you're free in space."

"Never been off-station. Never been on a ship, either," Binwa admitted.

"Anyhow, looks like the hatch was blocked from tight seal. I mean on purpose—I've sent you veed of it!"

"Yes. I should have expected this. This is part of it all, I'm afraid."

"Part of what?"

"Things happening. Comm channels I can't get to, and ships incoming but no one's talking to me. There's a Conference going on and I can't get feed on that, either. Security's tampered with, locking me out! I don't think they trust me, Geral, I see what they're up to!"

He sat; the board demanded ID.

"Binwa, you have to approve my biometrics, it says."

"Yes. They left me alone here and now I invoked Catastrophe Ops. I'll confirm you as Security, Acting Squad Leader. I got the key. Heck, I'll just make you Shift Security Leader. Sensors on!"

Geral paused, the sound of *Catastrophe Ops* bouncing around his thoughts, making him a little worried.

"I'm looking into the camera, straight-face, and got my left hand on the pad."

"I see this, Squad. Takes a moment—give me your full ID, number, and names."

He did the numbers and letters first, then said "Geral Jethri Quai-Hwang."

"Moment, Squad."

The screens lit up, followed by a shockingly loud click as something mechanical thunked in the walls near the hatch.

"You are live, Security Leader. Right now, there's you and me, and then there's the rest of the station. You're Security Lead. You can do almost anything. Wait, I need to take care of something. It may be a few minutes."

Probably has to go pee, Geral figured, *he's like that when he's nervous.*

Geral was used to waiting, but not to having this much information in front of him, open to him, with the time going from one minute to many.

But yes, he *did* see, there on one screen all the pressure points on the station, on a zoomable map-grid, and there, on another, the status of the doors, the pressure variations, water and fluid flow, the gravity variations. Also, *all* the reports, everyone's shift status, security stations, medical alerts, a blinking yellow triangle showing a guard status—

Two names he knew quite well, under guard in the hospital, on pregnancy watch. Tifney and Pettipi! Both of them? Both of the twins under guard? Both due multi-births?

He rolled the idea around in his head, remembering how they'd coralled him on First Orbit's Eve, the pair full of energy and inviting him to a quiet shindig, offering up a touch of *vya* and, after the *vya*, a long night on a bed full of them and them alone. The following shift-month they'd collected him individually a time or two—and then the Admin shifts changed and his moved to match Famy Binwa's. He'd wondered what happened.

The blood. They'd wanted his blood, that was what. And when they'd tested pregnant . . .

There was dread in his gut and he couldn't quite swallow it away.

· · · ·

BINWA DIDN'T TELL HIM what took a few minutes, but Geral knew it was far longer than that. He'd drilled down, peeking into private records, including the two women in hospital expecting multiple births. He found his own record, eventually, full of notations like "loner, no strong friendships, tractable if left to his own pursuits," but the cross-references to Senior Resource and Admin Alert made him worried, and the multiple notes over time—*Transfuse only to Seniors and Blood Resource*—worried him more.

Other areas didn't open to him—but yes, the Seniors had their own shifts and apparently they'd added his mother to their number, for her records were all behind a security wall he couldn't breach.

He'd closed that file, tried to understand the rest of the boards in front of him, including the 3D station situation board.

"I am back," Binwa said, sounding winded. "What do you see?"

"Three ships," Geral said once he figured out what he was looking at. "Three ships closing this says."

There was a curse then, and an ugly sound, like muffled warning horns over and over, and then distant shivers in the fabric of the station. Inside the armory, panels flashed, lights dimmed, the status board showed blue blocks on the station map—every pressure door and hatch was sealed or sealing. The words GENERAL SECURITY LOCKDOWN were prominent.

Under that status a series of images flashed onto the screens, security cameras showing rotating views of corridors. The red lights showed—

"Where's Security? If this is a general lockdown, where's the rest of Security?" Geral tried the corridor cameras, finding nothing. The meeting rooms, though, were crowded.

"Never mind them, Geral, *you're* Security, because I can depend on you, and *they're* conspirators. All of them. The rest are . . . offline. They'll have to back down, now."

"Who?"

"There's a revolt, Geral. The Seniors are trying to sell the station to the cheesers and that's not in the Crew Compact. The station and all of us, they want to trade us so they can live forever. You and me and . . . the Seniors are locked in a room, and Admin, too. They were having their meeting, so I had to act. The Seniors made me do it! I've put out a call-in for the rest of the Service Squad to take over Security, but you're the only one's come to me, Geral. My mother's on their side, she says the *Envidaria* is over, done. Who believes that?"

Geral thought about it. There hadn't been an end date on the *Envidaria*, the arrangement. It was how they'd lived for hundreds of Standards. It was what made Jethri and Arin so important, and helped guide millions of lives . . .

"Control, Green Office. I mean—I don't think the *Envidaria* is over, Binwa. I don't! What should I do, then?"

"There's a loyalty oath on the screen, Geral. Accept it. Then we'll open the armory weapons bay, so you can repel boarders."

· · · ·

GERAL WAS, according to Famy, fully second in command now. The Seniors, the Security Squad, everyone had to listen to Binwa until this got fixed. Binwa had a copy of *The Crew Compact* open and was reading it out across the channels to them. Geral could hear him in the background, droning on, then emphasizing random words.

Geral'd left the anteroom, secured it so it would only open to him or on order from Binwa. He'd rushed to the inner armory and now, in the weapons bay, he was bathed in brightness.

The full-suits were there. All of them were there, including three brand-news that had Full test Green labels everywhere—new and never worn.

He hurried, stripped to basics, grabbed up one with a green tag showing shoulder and hip to toe ratios that ought to do, and squiggled his way in, knowing that the wrong that was happening was *really* wrong—all the suits here ought already to be on someone, all of them ought to be in position, *all* of them. Comes to worst, might be someone expecting this suit might come through the seal any minute—

But they weren't roused, were they? All the external packs were on the wall, weren't they, *and* all the guns?

Seemed strange that they wouldn't have grabbed the guns for a revolt. Seemed strange they could have grabbed the Bloodlines—that would be Ma, among others!—without bothering other services. But the alert was out and they weren't here, the regular crew, nor his.

"Squad Forty," he said to the mic even before his gloves clicked on seal, "this is Lead on Squad Forty, back-up not suited yet," he said, knowing that someone in Control ought to have a veed feed and see him standing alone and know what he meant. If someone was back-up to Squad Forty they were going to have to show soon, else . . .

"Squad Forty, confirmed. Watching for you to get under pressure. Pack M and L are assigned yours. If crew shows with my code, make them double up on extras."

But there *wasn't* anybody else. It would be him and Binwa, wouldn't it? Pack M was the full mobility unit with projectiles as well as lasers. It was a leader's unit—had some range on the jets, had some firepower he'd never tried, but supposed to be automatic. The suit should fit itself in when he got there, and the unit ought to heed him . . .

"Sealed," he said when he was, again seeing the squad room that ought to have sixteen people, empty but for him. The heads-up display came live, bringing almost too much information: local internal and external pressure and atmospheres, state of the connections and network, ammunition count, loitering time, battery state, and . . . empty slots where Squad Leader ought to have a squad.

"Control? Squad Forty prepped for EVA, grabbing packs."

Not much more to be said, with no one talking back and no one yet coming to be his backup.

He slapped the plate and walked through, lights coming up as he did. Earnestly wishing there was motion behind him, knowing there wasn't, he only quarter-turned to the plate on this side, where the pre-packs waited, patient as death, for their missions.

That slap was bordering wistful; the angled sliver of view showed the stark white of the two closest suits, hanging empty, before the scissors of the closing door left him even more alone.

"Two seals, Control. Mounting up."

"You are authorized to open to vacuum and deploy. You are authorized to use force; your weapons are live."

There were two hatches, one with pack rails and one without, and the packs sat there waiting. The hatch could take five at a time if need be—

Geral backed into Pack M, reaching overhead to pull himself up onto that slight saddle, his elbows and forearms resting on the U of the equipment, his legs on the stirrups. Quick motions clicked the umbilical on each side into the power systems and into the pack's extended environmental units.

"Pack M systems attached to Leader," a quiet voice told him. "Accept, please."

He did that, and Pack M let him know that Pack L was attaching to hard points, which he felt, and he took a deep breath. Now the view was augmented even further and all those points there on the left side were weapons far more powerful than a pistol. He shuddered with knowing he'd not armed things yet, and knowing he had too much power, anyway, for someone whose leading had mostly been to a spot at the bar and then open a door for bed and a roll, if he was lucky.

"Geral, we need you to occupy Bay Four. The other docks are under control from here, so they're secure . . . and I got Traffic's radio feeds locked up tight so they can't be involved—but if that ship gets to the dock, I can't stop them here—none of the other service units are responding. Security has gone over, they're on strike, too. They're all Revolutionists and we got to stop them. Hold Bay Four!"

"Confirm, Control. Hold Bay Four."

• • • •

HE BARELY NOTICED SPACE, space being what there was mostly except for the reality of the station and the need to be at a hard-to-reach location. His suit was quiet around him, but he heard his own breathing, kept reminding himself to follow the color-coded dots, to follow the easy-to-read blinking lights . . . but no, he shouldn't!

Resisting the urge to talk to himself about it, he said, "Control, you might want to turn off traffic control lighting. I can see where I'm going without."

"Will do. Might need to go silent so they can't monitor . . . I'm releasing all suit control to you, Geral. You're autonomous now."

Many of the flashing lights went away. The numbers on the side of the station's hull didn't, but the details of a docking collar would be harder to see with the station rotating into darkness, especially if there was someone between you and getting close enough to use ship lights to illuminate it.

Guidance. He could use some guidance here . . .

"Control?"

Silence.

Out there, suddenly, there was blackness as the local star was eclipsed, and then again, the light making him a shadow.

They'd never warned him about this kind of stuff, that he'd be a sharp spot on the hull, that resisting invasion gave the advantage to the people out there who wanted to take . . .

"Test, circuit open. Spadoni, please reply. Please initiate routine docking. . . . There's my echoes, Spadoni, you can hear me.

"Spadoni, we are coming to dock. Please turn guidance on. This is Carresens *AnnaV* on a scheduled shipment. I am Pilot In Charge Luchinda Eerik of the—"

Luchinda? His Luchee? It sounded just like her, it did, even across the years and, yeah, she was quick and sharp. A pilot? But there was trouble now . . .

Also, Control was on silence and had locked down Traffic's radio.

"This is Squad Forty. There's been riots and Revolutionists. We can't let you dock until there's an all-clear ordered. We may use any means to hold this docking bay. We have been authorized to use force, if required."

"If you fire on my ship I will return fire, Squad Forty."

"I know you will, Luchee," he said, "Just like you busted my nose, thank you."

A pause, not caused by the slow crawl of radio waves. He used it to maneuver his unit to one of the hard points. The dull red triangle glowed in outline on the left and he speared the arms-length metal pipe protecting the cabling into it, feeling the snap as it tightened, followed by inserting the cable into the blue circle on the right with a similar mechanical snap. Pack M and Pack L oriented themselves as the hardpoint locked; he was essentially an external gun turret now.

He should have heard confirmation from Control on that, but inside the suit everything matched up. Autonomous.

Through his faceplate he could see another eclipsed star, and then augments hit and he had targeting information on a ship coming nearly straight at him. The bad news was that they must have him now, as well, know that he was not speaking from a station defense battery, he was merely a stud locked upright on a bright hull, casting a shadow to infinity.

"Squad Forty, we are not looking for a fight. We're not Revolutionists, we're a trade ship. And I'm getting counter information from another source claiming that you have been misrouted and misinformed and are to be ignored. If you're Geral, you're a braver fool than I ever realized, facing down a ship with a suit!"

He heard that, breathed a curse that was loud in his own ears even if not broadcast.

"Control? What status? What support?"

He was clicking between comm broadcast channels furiously, the head's up display showing him active bands.

After a long pause, Binwa broke silence.

"I still hold Control. Security won't help. They want to give the station away, the whole station, Geral! Why's there three ships? At least one of those ships are what they've been waiting on. They want to send us all to Fromage Two. They're going to occupy the station . . . you got to stop them from getting in."

"Squad?" came Luchee's drawl.

"*AnnaV*, I'm sorry. My orders remain."

"Dammit, Geral, you're alone in a spacesuit and there's three ships out here."

"I'm on lockpoint," he managed. "I've got war units, Luchee. Are you in a battleship?"

"Can't discuss it, Squad Forty. You're going to have to move away from that dock. I hope you'll do it soon; my shift is due to end but I'm not allowed to leave docking incidents unresolved. I'm lighting up for rendezvous."

The faceplate showed two ghostly outlines now, the M unit's sensors showing where the approaching ships were, where . . .

There! A blot took shape exactly where the faceplate put it, stars going away, and then the blot took color and shape as brilliant points of light, some blinking to varying pulses and others just there.

Training recall came to him, the five blue lights circling the nose of the ship meaning *AnnaV* was headed right at him, the slow blinking red lights ringing the blue were the pods-heads, the apparent bright ring between the blue and the red was where *AnnaV*'s hull swelled to the pod points. More light now, and he was awash in it, the faceplate barely shielding him from the full intensity. The approaching ship slowed, loomed . . .

From the station channels:

"Squad Forty, you must stand down and return your aux-packs to the armory. Your training mission is over. Famy Binwa has been relieved of all command. Your loyalty oath is noted. You must return to the armory . . ."

Geral shivered. It was Famy's ma!

"Don't listen! They've breached this line, but we resist the revolution. Civilians cannot understand the dangers—"

"This is Vice Administrator Binwa. My son has been relieved of shift and staff command and is being removed from the control room. You are now under my direct orders, Geral Jethri. Return to station, place yourself under Security's protection. You will be escorted to upgraded quarters and this incident will be purged from your file."

There was a short pause before she spoke again, sharply.

"Geral Jethri?"

He swallowed, the promise of upgrades making his stomach clench, as he thought of the twins, both pregnant. His kids. His blood . . .

There came sounds of heavy breathing, and pounding, through the earset, then Famy Binwa's voice, loud.

"I'm loyal to the *Envidaria*. This is a breach—I will resist, I will eject, I will—"

Beneath Geral, the station lurched, vibration traveling through the taut cables locking him and his packs to the surface, shaking him and his suit against the strapping.

"Geral Jethri? Let me make your choice plain. Return to station and receive an upgrade. Continue this revolt and we will be rid of you."

Geral was still trying to understand. Famy. The Revolutionists. Forced labor on the cheese worlds. The—

"I am," he whispered, "under the command of Famy Binwa."

There was another lurch; this one smaller and more personal.

"Control?" Geral demanded, wondering if some unknown ship had managed a violent latch-dock out of his view. "Squad Forty reporting anomaly—"

His faceplate showed him a flashing: UNLOCK ALERT UNLOCK ALERT UNLOCK ALERT UNLOCK at the same time it showed a potential target not much bigger than him drifting away from the station, a tumbling figure, a . . .

His faceplate flashed a warning—power issues for the lockpoint.

A KLUNG shook him; distantly a station thruster showed power and the station twisted. Or he did.

Jettisoned. He'd been jettisoned!

Below him the station rolled and the faceplate echoed that, and now it showed him the station as a target, receding slowly.

Everyone he knew in the universe was out there, targets. Targets, if he was willing.

• • • •

HE'D TRIED THREE AIRLOCKS, chasing them as the station rotated. It was as if he didn't exist. His suit showed station comm circuits locked against him, and the last effort to close with the station had been met by a round of attitude jets, almost taunting him.

Working his suit kept him calm; he had to think hard about it, but it was a new suit and getting easier to use every minute.

Eventually, one of the ships disappeared beyond the bulk of the station; he could see portions of it as it docked, but wasn't in comm circuit.

The other two ships now rode in orbit between him and the station. One was, he knew, the *AnnaV*. The other he didn't know—

"Spacer Geral Jethri, this is *AnnaV*, offering to connect you with a recovery ship."

Luchee's voice was calm and quiet in his ear.

"Spacer? I'm a stationer. I can't . . ."

"You are a distressed spacer, discovered free-floating in an orbit you are unable to recover from under your own power. I can certify that. We can do that for you, Geral Jethri."

"But the station! I'm Service Squad, I'm supposed to . . ."

"They abandoned you, Geral Jethri. You're locked out."

He fought with himself. He had forty hours of air. Enough firepower, though, to . . .

Famy Binwa had trusted him. Famy had fooled him. Famy . . . had ejected without a suit . . .

Luchee took a breath.

"Either you're a distressed spacer or you're dead," she said flatly.

"I don't have anything . . ." He stuttered to a stop.

She didn't argue that point. His air showed thirty-eight-point-seven hours now.

"Geral, I'm going off-duty. My shift is ending. Be smart. I can arrange for pick-up, while I'm Pilot In Charge. That's all I can do. You need to make the choice.

"You need to save yourself."

Geral stared beyond the lurking ships, beyond the station's disorienting rotation against the background of a distant three-mooned planet.

There was silence for a while. When Luchee spoke again, it was like she'd woken him up from a drowse.

"Geral, we're docking next. We can't pick you up; if you're on-board when we dock, Spadoni will arrest you. They'll lock you up and take your blood and you won't even get points for it! You'll never be free!"

The station rotated under him.

"The other ship with us is not docking, Geral. Will you let them pick you up? She . . . they believe in the *Envidaria*. They live by it. They're free! They want to talk to you, Geral. I trust them. Remember, we said we weren't going to give blood to the Seniors. You promised me, Geral! We'll be in radio shadow now, be smart!"

The station's rotation was patient, unforgiving. *AnnaV*, in pursuit of a docking bay, slid into the bright side while he and his suit were in the darkness.

Geral was alone, as he often was. But . . .

He had a choice. He could be desperate for what wasn't going to happen, like Famy Binwa, or he could be like Jethri and Arin had been and make something happen. He could let the Seniors own him or he could . . .

"This is Spacer Geral Jethri Quai-Hwang. What ship?"

He asked as if he knew ships, which he didn't; as if the name mattered. He'd been prepared to fire upon them, an hour gone, and now . . .

A pleasant female voice filled the ether, carried by a strong, directional signal.

"This is Ship *Disian*. Geral Jethri, may we match velocity with you and bring you aboard? Please, call me *Disian*.

"Also," came the pleasant voice, with no sense of irony, "it would be good if you would turn off targeting mode and safe your weapons. We can rendezvous in ten minutes."

Geral flinched, shook his head at himself, and safed the weapons. The oxygen read-out on his faceplate said thirty-six-point-seven hours and he was free to watch it count down, if he really wanted to. Maybe the station would pull him in, right before the last. Maybe they'd decide they needed his blood too bad to let him go.

Or, maybe they wouldn't.

A deep breath then, and he used his jets, turning to admire the view, and the ship, approaching.

The oxygen countdown had begun to bore him and he realized that, despite it all, he was getting hungry.

"Yes, Ship *Disian*," he said eventually. "Thank you. Please come for me. This distressed spacer accepts your offer of aid."

About the Authors

CO-AUTHORS SHARON LEE and Steve Miller have been working in the fertile fields of genre fiction for more than thirty years, pioneering today's sub-genre of science fiction romance – stories that contain all the action, adventure and sense of wonder of traditional space opera, with the addition of romantic relationships.

Over the course of their partnership, Lee and Miller have written thirty-one novels, twenty-three in their long-running, original space opera setting, the Liaden Universe®, where honor, wit, and true love are potent weapons against deceit and treachery.

There are more than 300,000 Liaden Universe® novels in print; Liaden titles regularly place in the top ten bestsellers in *Locus Magazine*, the trade paper of the speculative fiction genres; twelve titles have been national bestsellers.

Liaden Universe® novels have twice won the Prism Award for Best Futuristic Romance, reader and editor choice awards from *Romantic Times*, as well as the Hal Clement Award for Best YA Science Fiction Novel, proving the appeal of the series to a wide range of readers.

Lee and Miller's work in the field has not been limited to writing fiction.

Sharon Lee served three years as the first full-time executive director of the Science Fiction and Fantasy Writers of America, and went on to be elected vice-president, and president of that organization. She has been a Nebula Award jurist.

Steve Miller was the founding curator of the University of Maryland's Science Fiction Research Collection. He has been a jurist for the Philip K. Dick Award.

Lee and Miller have together appeared at science fiction conventions around the country, as writer guests of honor and principal speakers. They have been panelists, participated in writing workshops, and given talks on subjects as diverse as proper curating of a cat whisker collection, techniques for creating believable characters, and world-building alien societies.

In 2012, Lee and Miller were jointly awarded the E.E. "Doc" Smith Memorial Award for Imaginative Fiction (a.k.a.` the "Skylark" Award), given annually by the New England Science Fiction Association to someone who has contributed significantly to science fiction, both through work in the field and by exemplifying the personal qualities which made the late "Doc" Smith well-loved by those who knew him. Previous recipients include George R.R. Martin, Anne McCaffrey, and Sir Terry Pratchett.

Sharon Lee and Steve Miller met in a college writing course in 1978; they married in 1980. In 1988, they moved from their native Maryland to Maine, where they may still be found, in a sun-filled house in a small Central Maine town. Their household currently includes three Maine coon cats.

Steve and Sharon maintain a web presence at korval.com

Novels by Sharon Lee & Steve Miller

THE LIADEN UNIVERSE®: *Agent of Change * Conflict of Honors * Carpe Diem * Plan B * Local Custom * Scout's Progress * I Dare * Balance of Trade * Crystal Soldier * Crystal Dragon * Fledgling * Saltation * Mouse and Dragon * Ghost Ship * Dragon Ship * Necessity's Child * Trade Secret * Dragon in Exile * Alliance of Equals * The Gathering Edge * Neogenesis * Accepting the Lance * Trader's Leap*

Omnibus Editions: *The Dragon Variation * The Agent Gambit * Korval's Game * The Crystal Variation*

Story Collections: *A Liaden Universe Constellation: Volume 1 * A Liaden Universe Constellation: Volume 2 * A Liaden Universe Constellation: Volume 3 * A Liaden Universe Constellation: Volume 4*

The Fey Duology: *Duainfey * Longeye*
Gem ser'Edreth: *The Tomorrow Log*

Novels by Sharon Lee

THE CAROUSEL TRILOGY: *Carousel Tides * Carousel Sun * Carousel Seas*
   Jennifer Pierce Maine Mysteries: *Barnburner * Gunshy*

Pinbeam Books Publications

Sharon Lee and Steve Miller's indie publishing arm

• • • •

ADVENTURES IN THE LIADEN Universe®: *Two Tales of Korval * Fellow Travelers * Duty Bound * Certain Symmetry * Trading in Futures * Changeling * Loose Cannon * Shadows and Shades * Quiet Knives * With Stars Underfoot * Necessary Evils * Allies * Dragon Tide * Eidolon * Misfits * Halfling Moon *Skyblaze * Courier Run * Legacy Systems * Moon's Honor * Technical Details * Sleeping with the Enemy * Change Management * Due Diligence * Cultivar * Heirs to Trouble * Degrees of Separation * Fortune's Favor * Shout of Honor * The Gate that Locks the Tree * Ambient Conditions * Change State * Bad Actors*

Splinter Universe Presents: *Splinter Universe Presents: Volume One * The Wrong Lance*

By Sharon Lee: *Variations Three * Endeavors of Will * The Day they Brought the Bears to Belfast * Surfside * The Gift of Magic * Spell Bound * Writing Neep*

By Steve Miller: *Chariot to the Stars * TimeRags II*

By Sharon Lee and Steve Miller: *Calamity's Child * The Cat's Job * Master Walk * Quiet Magic * The Naming of Kinzel * Reflections on Tinsori Light*

105

THANK YOU

Thank you for your support of our work.
Sharon Lee and Steve Miller